Gems
of the
Valley

RAANA SAMI

Copyright © 2024 Raana Sami
All rights reserved
First Edition

Fulton Books
Meadville, PA

Published by Fulton Books 2024

ISBN 979-8-89221-447-6 (paperback)
ISBN 979-8-89221-448-3 (digital)

Printed in the United States of America

CHAPTER 1

The Celebration

It was a celebration, a one-of-a-kind joyous occasion of welcoming the new year. For the people in the valley of Kunar, spring marked the coming of festivities. It was a unique populace with its cheerful traditions and distinct individuals. Kunar Valley was surrounded by the mighty snow-capped Himalayan range. Rich in biodiversity, these mountains boasted climates ranging from tropical at the base to perennial snow and ice at the highest elevations. This captivating landscape was home to rare animals such as the snow leopard, Himalayan *tahr*, and musk deer. The people of the valley embraced spring with prayers and processions, all unfolding at the highest plateau outside the village. It was a time of nightlong dancing, enjoyed by young and old, women and men alike. And for young adults, it was the season to fall in love.

Gul's expression showed consternation. "Wow! What an amazing article!"

The five girls, all of similar age, gathered in the spacious bedroom upstairs. The room was well-lit with lamps and aided by a bright skylight. However, what truly caught one's attention was the French door opening onto the balcony, overlooking the valley below. Most of the girls were already dressed up in their typical traditional black flowing robes, which drifted through the air with the balcony's breeze. The robes were gathered at the waist with broad beaded belts known as kaftans. This traditional attire was a staple for the people of Kunar during ceremonies and festivals. The girls looked lovely, especially with the intricate embroidery done in bright, bold colors on their dresses.

"Something wrong?" inquired Palwasha, satisfied with what she saw in the mirror, clasping the last of many beaded colorful necklaces decorating her neck.

"Yaar, it's this article!" Gul remarked with a hint of annoyance in her tone.

"What about it?" Palwasha asked as she continued looking at herself in the mirror. "Hmmm, I think I'm all done. Ready, girls?" She finally turned around.

"Yes, yes, I am almost ready!" Zarmeena called out, quickly braiding her hair. "And what about you, Gul? What were you saying?" Zarmeena noticed an unmistakable look on Palwasha's face, as if she wanted recognition for her efforts in front of the mirror. "You look lovely," Zarmeena added quickly, turning her attention back to Gul.

Gul finally tore her gaze away from the engrossing magazine and looked up with a grin spreading across her face.

"You always look lovely, Palwa. You don't need us to say it."

Palwasha grinned and, with sudden confidence, began striking a pose as if she were modeling for a photoshoot. "That I know." She winked at her sister and cousin then plopped herself down on a floor cushion. "Gul, tell me again, what have you been so irked about?"

Gul nodded toward the magazine. "The article, Palwasha. How many times do I have to tell you?"

"Yes…and?" Palwasha questioned, looking at her sister.

"They have written about us," Gul explained.

"About us?" Palwasha sat up, evidently surprised as she looked around at everyone. "What do you mean? Here! Show it to me!" She sprang forward and almost snatched the magazine from her sister's hands. "This is exciting! Wait! Does this mean we are famous?" she chirped and continued reading out the rest of the article from where Gul had left off. "The Kunari people are indigenous to the district of Baltistan, located in the North Frontier region of Pakistan. They speak the Kunari language and are considered unique among the people of Pakistan. Historians have long regarded them as Pakistan's smallest ethno-religious group, practicing a religion that can be described as a form of ancient Hinduism."

Silence filled the room.

"Unique...*unique?*" Palwasha repeated the word as if trying to grasp its meaning. Growing increasingly agitated, she looked at her sister. Gul simply shrugged in response. Rolling her eyes, Palwasha began once again, this time in a louder tone for everybody to hear what the rest of the article had to say. "They are considered by some to have been descendants of migrants of North Euro-Asian stock, who were among the earliest migrants from West Asia to South Asia."

"Okay, I understand now. It seems we are being used to promote tourism!" Zarmeena interjected. "But the real question is, are we receiving any royalties?" Zarmeena now stood behind Palwasha, peering over her shoulder at the magazine directly. "Sometimes I feel like others see us as some species in a petri dish...like the world is looking at us through a microscope. I mean, they used the word 'stock' to describe us. How much worse can it get?" Zarmeena continued in a sarcastic tone.

"Shh, ladies. There's more," Palwasha said, looking around and quieting everyone.

"More!" the rest of the girls chimed in.

"Shhhh...not about us...Nooriabad is the next victim!" Palwasha responded.

"Okay, so what's new about Nooriabad?" one of the girls asked, growing impatient to go out.

Turning the page over, Palwasha continued, "The neighboring Noorani people of the Nooriabad Valley, near the border of Afghanistan, once had the same culture and practiced the same faith as the Kunari people—although with some differences. The first historically recorded Islamic invasion of their lands was by the Ghaznavis during the eleventh century. Nooriabad, under the influence of the invaders, had reverted to Islam during the eighteenth century. And while they still maintain some distinct customs, they are quite assimilated into the Islamic culture of greater Pakistan. In comparison, the Kunar of Baltistan have maintained their own separate cultu—"

"And you all are invited to observe them!" retorted Gul, cutting off Palwasha mid-sentence.

"Something like that!" muttered Palwasha under her breath, rolling the magazine and aiming it at the garbage bin. With a dull thud, it missed its mark. "Oh, darn!" Getting up, she picked up the magazine and placed it on the dresser. Looking around the room, she grabbed her colorful beaded cap, carefully adjusting it on her head, and checked herself in the mirror. She loved what she saw. "Great. Come on, let's go, girls! The world is clearly waiting to be dazzled by our song and dance, and I am least bothered about that stupid article!"

"You're forgetting the most important thing," Zarmeena remarked, looking at Palwasha with a mischievous smile on her lips.

"What?" Palwasha asked, hurriedly checking herself in the mirror. Palwasha was quite vain about her looks, but her heart was in the right place.

"The boys, Palwasha…ready to dazzle the world and the boys!" Zarmeena laughingly completed her sentence, batting her eyes at Gul and Palwasha.

"Huh…nah, I don't know what you're talking about," Palwasha snickered, turning around to look at her sister. "Coming, Gul?"

Gul had suddenly gone quiet.

"Gul?" Palwasha urged.

"Yes, yes, I am coming! You girls go ahead. Let me just put away my books!" She quickly turned and started picking up her books which were strewn across her bed.

Gul was preparing for her CSS exams, and the registration had started with the looming date. She just needed to submit the registration form. Looking at it, it was almost complete except for one last detail, right at the bottom of the page. The blank dotted line stared up at her. "Baba," she murmured affectionately to herself, the whole scene playing out in her mind.

CHAPTER 2

The Jirga

Fourteen-year-old Gul and her sister Palwasha stood alongside their mother and father at the *jirga*. The atmosphere was charged with intense discussions, occasional shouting, and moments of complete silence. Gul could hear her heart pounding loudly, fearing that someone might notice. Her father, Pasha, stood up, towering in his full height. He was a handsome man with kind eyes, his expression serious. A hush fell over the large group as he raised his hand. Pasha commanded respect not only because of his financial stability but also because he was held in high regard by the community. As an herbalist, he had inherited knowledge from his father and was always available to offer advice and assistance. He harbored a strong desire for the people of the community and the valley to embrace progress and development, ensuring that they wouldn't be left behind. He understood that without keeping pace with the outside world, their future would be bleak, their existence reduced to a mere footnote on the country's map, known only as an obscure indigenous relic speculated upon by outsiders.

"Please...please...we've had a lot of discussion going in circles...but getting nowhere. Instead, we are wasting time," his voice almost pleading as he looked around at the faces before him.

"Wasting...precious time, *Pasha*?" A hefty man with a roundish face stood up, Iqbal, a close friend of Pasha's. "How do you think we are wasting time?" he inquired, waving his arm toward the jirga. His tone carried a hint of annoyance.

Pasha smiled at his friend, unfazed by Iqbal's questioning tone. "Iqbal, I am not talking about this particular jirga meeting. It's not wasting time," he clarified.

"Then?" Iqbal interrupted, growing impatient.

"Well, let me just put it this way," Pasha continued, looking around and speaking in a soft but firm tone. "The precious time of our girls is going to waste. Their future is on hold. It is not only the boys' right, but the girls of our valley should be allowed to pursue higher studies. They would ultimately be the ones to bring about change in our society. We cannot keep them shut out from the rest of the world anymore. The world around us is moving at a fast pace, and we all need to move forward together. Give the girls their due right. Let them study, let them work. I urge you all to embrace that… please!"

There was complete silence as Pasha's words sank in.

He could sense that his message had made an impact. He continued, "Tell me, do you want people from outside the valley to treat us like aliens? We have *one* chance to normalize our people, to practice and enhance our children's outlook while preserving our culture. Let us seize this opportunity!"

There was complete silence except for the crackling of the burning twigs in the fire pit that had been set up for the *jirga*. The summer evenings in the valley could be a bit chilly.

Pasha could feel his wife's cold hand on his own, and she whispered nervously, "What now?"

The decision of the eldest member of the *jirga*, Jahan Khan, a man in his eighties who was leading the meeting, would be the final verdict.

The two girls were entrenched in silence, sensing perfectly well that their future as well as the future of the rest of the girls in the valley depended on the old man they were gazing at from a distance. Palwasha, shifting nervously, went to sit on a big boulder near the clearing that led to the walking trail. Gul joined her.

"What are they talking about?" she whispered in Palwasha's ear.

"Don't know," Palwasha replied, shaking her head, her gaze fixed on the group of old men. Both girls understood what was being discussed. The men surrounding Jehan Khan were now talking animatedly. For Pasha and his girls, who were concerned, it seemed that time had slowed down, and the men with white beards huddled together, taking an awfully long time to deliberate. The conversation among them ceased, and all the attendees directed their attention toward Jehan Khan. He pointed his weathered staff toward Pasha and gestured for him to come forward. Pasha suddenly felt rooted to the ground, his wife giving him a slight nudge.

"You must go, Pasha," she whispered.

Glancing at her with a nervous smile, Pasha scanned the faces of his friends and family as he approached Jahaan Khan. Jahaan Khan stood up shakily, and his grandson moved quickly to support him, but Jahaan Khan waved him off. Instead, he began to lean on Pasha while embracing him. Pasha kissed the back of Jahaan Khan's hand in respect, knowing that the future of the women of the Kunaar Valley was sealed for the better.

Holding Pasha's hand in his, Jahaan Khan raised it up like a referee in a boxing ring.

In a loud, booming voice, he declared, "To the people, freedom is the glory of God. Let's all benefit from that!"

Gul and Palwasha were mesmerized. They could feel the excitement in their bones, the promise of a better future.

Chapter 3

Stars Alight

A decade had passed, and attitudes had naturally changed. Suddenly, the noise of a rock hitting the bedroom floor startled Gul out of her reverie. A small pebble had come flying through the French door into the room.

"What? Who's there?" Gul exclaimed. She rushed out onto the balcony, looking down. "Najeeb! What are you doing? You could have hit me!"

But instead of answering, Najeeb waved. "And also, you're not supposed to still be here, Gul." Grinning, Najeeb waited for her answer.

Gul held the form in her hand, which flapped like a caged bird. Afraid it might fly off, she carefully folded the form. "Well?" she inquired, a tad bit annoyed.

"Well, what?" Najeeb laughed, clearly enjoying Gul's discomfort. "No worries, Gul. Palwasha already gave me the green light." He looked up and shaded his eyes with his hand.

"Palwasha is an idiot. And why aren't you with the rest of the group up there? You're not supposed to be here either," Gul remarked, jerking her head in the direction of the animated sounds of music and laughter.

Najeeb was Gul and Palwasha's cousin, three years older than them. They were good friends, and Najeeb had always admired Gul's down-to-earth and resilient nature even though he seldom expressed it. Over time, their friendship had grown stronger. Najeeb had majored in public relations and mineralogy, and he had cleared the CSS Examinations. Now he was serving as an assistant commissioner in the District of Chitral.

"Okay, fine." He backed away. "And listen, do you remember our plan for tonight?"

"Yeah, yeah. The barn. I remember. Now will you just go?" she shouted at him as he lingered. Giving Gul a thumbs-up, Najeeb went to join his friends.

Finally, Gul went back inside and opened the drawer of her desk and put the form inside, locking it shut. With a last quick look in the mirror, she hurried downstairs, taking two steps at a time. She ran onto the veranda, crossing the sprawling expanse of green and climbing the earth-filled steps to the clearing where all the action was taking place. It was an open glade with the mountains as the backdrop.

The orange flame of the bonfire raged in the pit, and men dressed in *shalwar kameez* and *pakol* hats—a soft, round-topped woolen hat adorned with a single feather in the middle—huddled around it. The participants, young and old, danced to a unique musical piece consisting of twelve distinct tunes unlike any form of music found in Pakistan. The air was filled with laughter, and the mouthwatering aroma of the barbecue being prepared.

On her way to the spot where her friends and Palwasha were gathered, Gul paid her respects to the elders who were enjoying watching the youngsters dance.

"There she is!" Zarmeena almost shrieked with excitement, moving away from the group she was in. "You're late, Gul."

Zarmeena ran toward her, meeting her halfway. Coming to a halt in front of Gul, she exclaimed, "You're missing all the excitement!"

Gul and Zarmeena walked toward the group, and Gul noticed Palwasha talking with a lady reporter about something. While the rest of the girls were talking about the article in the magazine, Gul's attention was drawn toward where her sister was.

"That's good. Yes, yes. Just turn a little to the right. Hold it…chin up a bit." The reporter moved around Palwasha, clicking away her pictures. Palwasha being Palwasha thoroughly enjoyed the attention.

"What is she doing?" Gul muttered and unable to contain herself, without hesitation, she jumped in between Palwasha and the camera. "What's happening, Palwa? What do you think you're doing?" She gave a slight tug at her sister's hand and turned to the reporter.

"And what do you think you're doing taking her pictures?" Gul questioned, almost ready to snatch the camera away from the girl's hand.

Palwasha stepped in, anxiously trying to diffuse the awkwardness. "Gul, she's my friend—Anoosha. She's a freelance writer, and she's writing an article about our festival."

Tactfully ignoring Gul's heated behavior, Anoosha extended her hand. "Palwasha asked me to take some shots of her on my DSLR. They're not being published anywhere." She smiled reassuringly.

"Oh!" Gul felt embarrassed, quickly covering it up with a quick smile. "Welcome, Anoosha. Sorry about the outburst," she said sheepishly.

"No worries," Anoosha replied. "Your sister and the rest of the girls have been showing me around and explaining everything about the festival. It's so amazing. And what the girls told me totally took me by surprise!"

Curious, Gul inquired, "And what was that?"

By this time, the girls had settled comfortably on the grass. "Well, while I was asking Palwasha about the community, we came to the topic of education, and she told me the literacy rate is almost ninety-four percent now."

Gul looked at her with pride in her eyes, and before she could say anything, Zarmeena chimed in. "Yes, it is. And we are all very proud of Gul here. She's a role model for all the girls in the valley to pursue education." She patted Gul on the back.

Anoosha and the rest of the group turned their attention to Gul. Gul glared at Zarmeena, slightly blushing. "Oh, it's nothing, really," Gul replied, thinking about how she had yet to take the CSS Exam.

These girls are hyping me up as if I've aced it, she thought.

"Hey, c'mon, tell me about what you're studying!" Anoosha urged Gul, sensing that she was underselling her accomplishments.

Palwasha, who had stayed quiet till then, blurted, "She's preparing for the CSS exams!"

Anoosha's was taken aback, feeling a newfound respect for Gul. "This is news! It's definitely the topic of my next article!"

By now, the barbecue was ready, and plates brimming with juicy, aromatic meat, accompanied by bread and fresh fruits, were being passed around.

"This smells and looks delicious!" Anoosha exclaimed, delighting in the flavors as she dug into the food.

The dancing had come to a halt, and the air was filled with hushed conversations, bursts of laughter, and the intoxicating scent of jasmine. The evening felt perfect, wrapped in an enchanting atmosphere. Anoosha's gaze wandered and settled on a young man sitting by the bonfire, engrossed in playing the flute. His eyes were closed, surrendering himself to the melodies that flowed from his instrument. He and his flute seemed to share an unspoken language, harmonizing as one. "Who is that?" Anoosha whispered, captivated by the musician.

"That's our family friend Najeeb," Palwasha responded, her voice barely above a whisper. They exchanged their words discreetly, not wanting to disrupt the captivating flute melody.

Anoosha strained her eyes, attempting to recognize his features amidst the flickering firelight. "I think I remember him. I met him at the AC Office in Chitral."

"Oh, really?" Palwasha replied, a mischievous twinkle in her eyes. "Well, that's not surprising, considering he is the assistant commissioner in Chitral." The group erupted into laughter at her playful annoyance.

Refocusing her attention on Gul, Anoosha probed, "You were telling me about the spring season and the festival."

Gul glanced at the small tape recorder that Anoosha had switched on and continued her narrative. "Well, our festivals are closely tied to the four seasons. For example, today's celebration marks the arrival of spring and the commencement of the harvest season. And as autumn sets in, we have the Month of the Falling Leaves, which also brings another festive occasion. Nowadays, we've introduced a community-wide polo event during these festivities."

Anoosha's interest piqued as she soaked in the cultural customs described by Gul. It was more than a mere recitation; Anoosha was immersed in the experience unfolding around her. "And what about the remaining two seasons? What are they called?" Anoosha inquired, eager to learn more.

By now Gul was feeling at ease with Anoosha. She continued with more fervor, "Anoosha, you should visit here during winters, it is magically beautiful, the winter is called the Big Cold, which is followed by the Month of Melting Snow. And then we embrace the Moon Month, signaling the beginning of a new cycle," Gul explained, painting a vivid picture with her words.

The sound of the flute ceased, giving way to the lively pounding of drums just as Gul concluded her narrative. The young men and women began to gather around the fire, forming a circle with the girls on one side and the boys on the other.

Gul, Palwasha, their cousin Zarmeena, and the rest of the girls enthusiastically joined the group, swaying and moving in sync with the pulsating beat of the drums. Anoosha skillfully captured the captivating scene through the lens of her camera. The valley now resonated with the rhythmic thumping of drums, growing louder and more vibrant with each beat. The resounding echoes filled the air, reverberating throughout the valley and beyond.

CHAPTER 4

The Barn

"Najeeb…Najeeb," a voice hissed through the shrubs.

Stopping in his tracks, Najeeb strained his eyes in the darkness, searching for the source of the voice. "Who's there?" he whispered. "Come out, show yourself!"

"It's me!" the voice whispered back.

"Me is not a name," Najeeb replied.

"Come on, Najeeb. It's me!"

The rustling of the shrubs finally revealed Gul. A dry twig was sticking out of her thick braided hair. She quickly brushed off the dirt and dry leaves from her dress then jumped over the shrub with a smile. Najeeb gently pulled out the twig from her hair.

"Why are you hiding here?" he asked, walking slowly up the gravel path toward the barn.

Ignoring his question, Gul retorted, "Where have you been? I've been waiting behind that bush for almost an hour!" She was panting and out of breath, struggling to keep up with Najeeb.

"I thought you'd want more time with your new friend," he said, slowing down to let Gul catch up.

Looking at her condition, he smiled lopsidedly. "You need to get fit, you know. Too much sitting and doing nothing does that to you," he teased, offering her a water bottle.

Glancing up at him, she took the bottle and drank deeply. "I'm fine. And you have longer legs. And I don't just sit around all day.

And by the way, you said midnight," she replied, gasping out her words.

Najeeb continued walking but soon realized Gul wasn't beside him. He turned back and walked towards her, a mischievous glint in his eyes. "Gul?" he called. "And oh! I thought people turned into something ugly at midnight, especially beautiful girls! Didn't want to meet a bloodthirsty witch—that's why I took my time coming."

"Ha ha ha," Gul mimicked his laugh, giving him a friendly push.

It was a beautiful moonlit night. At this hour, they could hear the distant beat of drums echoing through the valley.

"They're still at it," Najeeb remarked. "Burning the midnight bonfire." He chuckled.

"No, burning their calories." Gul giggled softly.

Grinning, Najeeb pulled out a long metal key. They had reached the barn, the steps leading up to the door creaking under their weight. Inserting the key into the keyhole, he glanced at Gul.

"I've got something to show you." With a light click, he turned the key and pushed the door open then switched on the flashlight he was carrying. Gul followed closely behind him.

"I know you wanted to show me something. Otherwise, why would I be here?" Gul shot back.

"Let's be real. You'd be here even if I didn't have anything to show you," Najeeb answered without missing a beat, at the same time throwing the beam of light around the barn.

"Hmmm." Gul thought it best not to retort. Once inside, she took the flashlight from Najeeb, aiming the beam directly at his eyes. Indignation marked her face as she spoke. "Just to make this clear, this late-night rendezvous in this shabby old barn"—she gestured with the flashlight in a zigzag motion—"is purely out of curiosity."

Almost tripping over something, she let out a shriek. "*And what on earth is that?*" Her fright was evident, and she seemed ready to jump out of her skin. On the floor lay a long rectangular shape covered in a tarpaulin. Gul crouched against the wall, her voice trembling. Her eyes darted toward the door as if fearing that someone might witness them uncovering a corpse. Shuddering, she quickly kicked the door shut. "Najeeb, tell me the truth. Are you in trouble or something?" Fear widened her eyes, and she awaited a response. However, Najeeb remained silent, engrossed in unzipping the tarpaulin cover. "I asked you something. Is something wrong?" Gul's voice was laden with genuine concern.

"No, nothing's wrong," he calmly replied.

"No?" Gul's fear was palpable at this point.

Attempting to console her, Najeeb realized her genuine worry. "Hey, hey, it's okay." He then removed the cover, revealing a big rectangular box.

Gul's eyes were fixed on the object. "A coffin?"

"No, you idiot. It's a cardboard box containing something truly amazing." Najeeb's response carried a hint of exasperation. "I assure you, I'm not in cahoots with a murderer." He fully expected Gul to anticipate something grotesque inside the box, considering the countless practical jokes he had played on her in the past. "Here, hold the flashlight." Handing her the torch, he swiftly tore off the masking tape with a slash of his knife.

Peering cautiously into the box, he beckoned Gul. "Hey, don't just stand there—help me with this."

Gul's eyes widened in disbelief as she directed the beam of light inside. Lost for words, she looked at Najeeb, pleasantly surprised. "Oh my! Oh wow!" The shiny metallic tubes of a telescope gleamed under the beam of the flashlight as they both moved forward, kneeling down. "Is it really what I think it is?" Gul asked, fingering the apparatus lightly.

Najeeb nodded with a quick smile. "Yes, it is. But be very careful. Just hold the light for me and I'll take it out." Removing the bubble wrap, Najeeb handed Gul a stand. "Can you set up this stand for me?" he requested. Excitedly, Gul quickly assembled it outside under the barn's porch.

Observing Najeeb cradling the telescope like a precious baby, she couldn't help but comment, "This is truly a beauty. When did you buy it?"

"I didn't buy it." Najeeb shook his head, carefully balancing the telescope in one arm and shining the torchlight for Gul.

"Huh?" Gul gave him a questioning look.

"I borrowed it from one of my friends at work," Najeeb explained, adjusting the sleek and shiny instrument on the stable tripod stand.

Seated on the veranda steps, Gul tilted her head toward Najeeb. Resting her chin on her hand, she remarked, "Your friend must be quite generous. I wouldn't lend this beauty to just anyone, not even Palwasha."

Najeeb peered at Gul through the gap between the stand and the body of the telescope while tightening the bolts. "Oh, and I thought you would take my name instead of Palwasha." Najeeb grinned, sitting on his haunches. His other hand rested loosely on the lens, waiting for her reaction.

Thank God it's nighttime, she thought to herself, her face turning red.

Trying to retort with a smart remark, Najeeb burst into laughter, thoroughly enjoying her nervousness. It was a rare sight, and Gul, realizing how childishly she was behaving, joined in the laughter. "By the way, why did your friend lend it to you? Doesn't he want it anymore?" Gul inquired curiously.

Her remark made Najeeb get up and extend his hand toward her, motioning for her to get up. Ignoring the gesture, she stood up without his help. Najeeb shrugged, smiling to himself, and ignored her muttering under her breath. Gul was already leaning forward, peering through the lens.

Seeing this, Najeeb came to stand beside her and said, "Take your time to adjust and get used to the eyepiece."

Following his instructions, Gul cautiously looked through the eyepiece, making sure not to bump the telescope while holding it with her other hand. She took her time trying to focus, and complete silence ensued for thirty seconds.

Growing slightly impatient, Najeeb remarked, "You must be mesmerized." But there was no response. "Well, tell me what you see?!" Najeeb urged her, thinking she might not understand what she was looking at. "The moon with its—"

"Nothing!" Gul cut off Najeeb midsentence, a look of exasperation on her face. "There's nothing! It's just black!" Surprised by her outburst, Najeeb moved forward to look through the lens and adjust the focus. "Well?" Gul impatiently asked him, still refusing to move from her spot as if the telescope would fly off if she budged.

"Would you mind taking your hand off the lens, please?" Najeeb requested.

"What? What hand?" Gul inquired, confused. As she followed his gaze, she realized she had been covering the lens with her hand. Both of them burst out laughing.

Shaking his head, Najeeb motioned for her to come forward and said, "Look through it now."

A feeling of awe and wonder swept over Gul as she peered through the telescope. She was rendered speechless. The moon, with all its radiant beauty, appeared like a giant shiny globe suspended in the starry darkness, just within her reach.

"Cat got your tongue?" Najeeb teased.

"It's just…amazing," Gul finally managed to say, still mesmerized by the view. She remained glued to the telescope, holding her breath and afraid to blink, fearing she would lose sight of this captivating beauty. "It's the supermoon today, isn't it?" Gul was still fixated on the telescope.

"Yes, and it's called the Pink Moon," Najeeb added.

Both of them took turns enjoying the breathtaking sight.

Still observing the celestial beauty, Gul, with a wistful tone, said, "You know, if I had enough money to spare, we could build an observatory right here. It's the perfect spot."

"Hmm," Najeeb responded, "I do agree, but for now, I think it should remain our secret."

Their relationship was peculiar. They were good friends, yet their closeness gave the impression to the elders of both families that there was something more between them. Speculations of a budding romance had started circulating within the community. However, both of them vehemently denied it. In fact, Gul had argued with Najeeb, accusing him of spreading such rumors.

"Hold your horses, Gul! Do you really think I'm that kind of person?" He felt angry and disappointed. "I would never ruin your reputation with insinuations and rumors," he had argued, and that put an end to the topic.

CHAPTER 5

The Den

"Ten thousand dollars, that's how much!"

The dull light from the lanterns made the rubies in his hands seem like burning embers.

"It's not even my best," the forty-seven-year-old dealer smiled, revealing his perfect white teeth. His eyes shimmered under a set of thick, bushy eyebrows, much like the stones he had on display. He took a long puff from the hookah and then tightly clasped his hand around the glittering stones, swiftly stowing them away as if performing a magic trick for his audience. "I show the best pieces to people who have a bag full of cash." A hush fell over the small group of men gathered around the lamp in Khalil's shop. Other gemstones were scattered on white sheets of paper—sapphires, emeralds, citrines, and aquamarines—creating an ambience of a cave filled with treasures.

But the true prize was the rubies.

Initially extracted from the remote mountain ranges of the Himalayas, which skirted along the Afghan-Pakistan border, rubies of such quality were then smuggled over treacherous terrains that crossed the valley of Baltistan and into the oldest gem markets in Peshawar. These stones had the power to transform a beggar into royalty, and Khalil was an example of such transformation. Other gem dealers in the market wondered how a man who had struggled to survive just a few months earlier was now conducting business with gems worth hundreds of thousands of dollars. Khalil had built a house in Peshawar, dealing in smuggled goods, especially gems.

Today, he received an unexpected message: "Polo match."

It was written on the back of a receipt delivered by a food delivery boy who came with a pizza he hadn't ordered. After dealing with the customers in his shop, he went into his adjacent house.

There, on the table, was a large box of pizza.

"Can't let it go to waste," he said to himself. He wouldn't pass up a slice of pizza even if he wasn't hungry. "Rehmat…Rehmat!" Khalil called out as a fifteen-year-old boy appeared.

"Yes, yes, boss?" he inquired with an earnest expression on his face.

Khalil had taken in Rehmat when he was just eight years old. At that time, the boy was working at a roadside hotel, washing dishes and tending to customers. The little boy reminded Khalil of his own son back in Balakot.

"Would you like to come and live with me?" Khalil had asked.

The young Rehmat had no family; his father and sister were killed in an IED blast, and his mother had passed away during his birth. Rehmat, while working at the hotel during the day, used to sleep under a bench in the park near the hotel. "You can make tea for me, clean my house, and jeep," Khalil added, patting the boy affectionately on the head. Rehmat did not hesitate a bit. Khalil had given money to the hotel owner, and now, Rehmat was living with Khalil.

They were there for each other like father and son.

"Did you order this pizza?" Khalil asked, a bit sternly but with a twinkle in his eyes and a smile playing on his lips. He always loved joking around with the boy.

"No, no, boss, I thought you did," the boy said, coming forward and opening the box. "This sure looks good." His mouth watered at the appetizing sight.

"Hmm, I must have ordered it then and forgot about it," Khalil remarked with a chuckle, pulling out a chair and sitting down, enjoying the look on Rehmat's face. "Go get some plates and the large Pepsi bottle." The boy's face broke into a large grin, and he quickly ran out to get the cutlery.

Khalil, for a moment, was lost in thought.

"I guess the arrival of the pizza means the arrival of a guest from far off," Khalil muttered.

He was prepared for this moment.

The sudden hiss of gas escaping from the Pepsi bottle jolted him back to reality.

Rehmat had already put two large pieces of pizza on their individual plates and was pouring Pepsi into their glasses. "Just give me half," Khalil requested. The boy complied and took a bite into the large pizza slice.

"This is really yummy," he remarked with his mouth full.

"Rehmat?" Khalil said quietly.

"Yes, boss? Do you need anything?" the boy inquired, ready to dash to attend to his boss's needs.

"No, no…listen, Rehmat. I am expecting a guest tonight, but he won't be staying the night. In fact, we won't be staying the night," Khalil declared, piquing Rehmat's curiosity.

Rehmat's eyes widened with surprise as he eagerly asked, "What do you mean?"

For a brief moment, Khalil remained silent, the room filled with nothing but the steady ticking of the round wall clock. Taking a deliberate sip from his glass, Khalil gazed at Rehmat, his expression pensive. Finally, he spoke, his voice filled with a sense of adventure. "We're heading to Chitral to attend the polo match."

The room fell into a stunned silence, punctuated only by the gentle crackling of melting ice in the glass.

Rehmat couldn't believe his ears.

The thought of going to Chitral had never even crossed his wildest imagination. Rehmat knew that Khalil would never joke about an opportunity like this, a chance to witness the world-famous polo match. Silent excitement surged within him as he quickly rose from his seat, his mind racing with thoughts. The pizza and Pepsi were now the least of his concerns.

He had bags to pack.

Leaving the room in a rush, Rehmat prepared for the journey ahead, feeling a sense of restrained anticipation building in the pit of his stomach. Meanwhile, Khalil pushed his half-eaten plate aside, downing the soda in one large gulp. Glancing at his watch, he realized it was already 6:00 p.m.

Only six more hours till midnight.

As the date on the calendar triggered memories, Chitral and Kunar emerged from the hidden depths of Khalil's mind. These two places had a way of captivating his thoughts. Reflecting on the beautiful valley of Kunar, he recalled describing it as an oasis of cherry and apricot trees nestled between towering snow-covered mountains.

"Pasha..." he whispered to himself, his heart racing.

The reminiscence stirred restlessness within him.

Solitude had always been both a blessing and a curse for Khalil. Agitated, Khalil rose to his feet and began pacing the room, his mind consumed with restless thoughts. Suddenly, his eyes fell upon a painting hanging on the back wall. With a gentle touch, he pushed the painting aside, revealing a hidden wall panel. Slowly, he opened the panel, revealing a dimly lit passage illuminated by battery-powered bulbs.

Hunching slightly, Khalil briskly walked down the passage, leading him to a spacious workshop concealed at the back of the house through an underground passage. From the front, no one would suspect the existence of this hidden workshop.

It was a closely guarded secret.

Inside the workshop, two men sat a few feet apart, absorbed in their work at their respective benches. Upon spotting Khalil, they nodded in acknowledgment and continued their tasks. Khalil approached their work area, inspecting their work with a discerning eye.

"You have to be extremely careful with this batch," Khalil warned, pointing to a pool of rough, uncut rubies scattered on a crumpled sheet of gray paper.

"So, Khalil," one of the workers seated behind a bench equipped with a versatile rotary tool for gem cutting inquired, "when do you expect the clients to return?"

Khalil remained silent, casting the inquisitive man an icy glare. The other man in the workshop understood the unspoken message and focused on his work, avoiding further discussion. Khalil nodded, addressing the first man, "The work should be impeccable. Pay close attention. The clients are particularly demanding this time." He lit a cigarette and settled onto a rigid square bed known as a *takht*.

"The machines you purchased, boss, are fantastic. They enhance the beauty of the stones even more," the man named Nazeer remarked.

Taking a long drag from his hookah, Khalil responded, "Ensure the cuts are flawless, Nazeer. Otherwise, these machines serve no purpose for us."

As the clock neared 11:00 p.m., the workshop closed for the night. Both men collected their wages and prepared to leave. Khalil handed them a thick roll of cash, along with some extra.

Surprised, Nazeer looked at Khalil and asked, "Why such a substantial amount of cash, boss? Aren't you planning to come in tomorrow?"

"You guys did an exceptional job today," Khalil praised, patting them both on the shoulders.

After the men left, he swiftly returned through the passage into his room, closing the panel behind him and adjusting the picture on the wall. He proceeded to his bedroom to prepare for the trip. Retrieving a folded muslin cloth from his pocket, he carefully unfolded it to reveal thirteen radiant red gems in his hand. With nimble fingers, he individually wrapped each ruby in the muslin cloth. Opening the built-in cupboard, he took out three exquisitely embroidered women's gowns known as *kahet* or *kamis*, featuring intricate needlework and mirror embellishments around the neckline, sleeves, and hem. He carefully removed the mirrors from the hems and sleeves, sewing the muslin-wrapped rubies in their place. Once secured, he glued the mirrors on top of the muslin cloth. He neatly folded the adorned garments along with a few more embroidered *kamis* and shawls, placing them inside a vibrant plastic bag.

"Boss! Boss," Rehmat's voice echoed from outside the door.

"Yes, Rehmat, come in. Are the baskets ready?" Khalil inquired.

"Yes, boss, they're ready. Take a look at how beautiful they turned out," Rehmat replied excitedly.

Khalil approached the table in the hall and beheld three magnificently decorated baskets on display.

"I have packed each basket just as you instructed," Rehmat said, pointing toward the exquisite display. One basket overflowed with sweets from the local bakery, meticulously arranged in vibrant red and green boxes. Another basket showcased an array of beautifully designed and colorful bangles. The third basket held a diverse assortment of fruits and nuts.

Smiling with satisfaction, Khalil turned to Rehmat. "Good job. Have you packed your belongings?" he inquired.

"Yes, boss. I have everything with me," Rehmat replied eagerly.

"Okay, good," Khalil responded. "Just go and get some rest. I will wake you up when it's time to leave."

"Thank you, boss," Rehmat replied, his face radiant with excitement.

Khalil returned to his room, switched off the light, and lay down on his bed. Sleep eluded him as thoughts raced through his mind.

Should I contact Pasha? Will he recognize me? These questions made Khalil restless and pondering late into the night.

The memories of his loved ones flooded his mind, intensifying the ache of loneliness within him. The emptiness in his heart remained, a constant reminder of the shattered fragments of his life, swallowed by the merciless earthquake that had snatched everything away.

Balakot, once his home, now lay in ruins—a devastating scene of destruction that shattered the illusions of stability and security. It was as if someone had forcefully swept everything he held dear off the table, leaving behind a jumble of broken pieces scattered across the floor. Unable to face the overwhelming loss, Khalil had vanished, disappearing from the lives of those who knew him. Nobody knew his whereabouts or had caught a glimpse of him. It was as if he had joined his family, his two sons and his wife, in both life and death, forever entwined in tragedy.

A soft tapping on his windowpane drew his attention, breaking his train of thought.

With the engine humming, Khalil and Rehmat loaded the baskets and bag of clothes into the back of the jeep. Rehmat settled himself in the back seat, surrounded by their carefully packed belongings. Khalil opened the front door and took his place in the passenger seat. The driver, already seated behind the wheel, greeted them with a nod and switched on the headlights, casting a beam of light into the darkness ahead.

The journey to Chitral had begun, the anticipation of the world-famous polo match filling the air. The jeep rumbled forward, its tires gripping the road as they ventured into the night, embarking on an adventure that held both excitement and unknown challenges.

CHAPTER 6

The Surprise

Dawn broke, casting a fresh and clear light that seeped through the curtains, bathing the room in a warm yellow glow. Gul had always adorned their bedroom window with wind chimes made of seashells. Today, like every other day, she woke to the delightful tinkling sound they produced. A smile brightened her face; she found solace in that gentle melody. Yet beneath her morning cheer, a lingering sense of unease began to crawl up her spine. Her exams were finally over, but now the agonizing wait for the results had begun. Gul thought aloud, *Not today. I'm going to make the most of this day. It's perfect for a bike ride.*

She had planned an outing with her cousin Zarmeena, lying in bed, she could hear her mother conversing with the household helper. Her parents were discussing a trip to Balakot, where they would visit her aunt and uncle. Stretching her arms lazily, Gul's gaze wandered to the bed against the opposite wall. It was impeccably made, the blanket neatly folded and stowed away, and the sheet flawlessly tucked as if no one had slept in it. Propping herself up on both elbows, she pondered over Palwasha. Over the past two months, with the assistance of some girls and under the guidance of their father, Palwasha had been aiding local women in establishing a small-scale manufacturing business. Handcrafted caps, hair beads for women, and embroidered kaftans were their main products. Palwasha, along with Anoosha, her reporter friend, had been tirelessly working alongside her sister at the workshop day in and day out. Despite her role as a reporter, Anoosha was wholeheartedly involved in every aspect of the project, and today was no different. Gul had urged Palwasha to take a day off, but her sister remained resolute in keeping her commitment to Anoosha; they were planning to give extra time for the project even on weekends.

"It's okay. You go ahead. You deserve a break," Palwasha tried to convince Gul.

"Palwasha, both of us need a break. One day won't make a difference. Someone else can step in for a day." But Palwasha refused to yield, and Gul reluctantly accepted defeat.

"It's all right, Gul," Palwasha consoled her. "Perhaps next time."

"Yeah…next time," Gul grumbled.

Glancing at the clock, Gul leapt out of bed—hastily straightening the covers and plumping up the pillows. *"Ugh! I'm going to be late!"* she muttered, swiftly changing into a long embroidered shirt and slacks. Gul was supposed to meet Zarmeena around eleven o'clock at the cable car station. They had planned a full day of hiking and biking to revel in the delightful weather. With her exams finally behind her, Gul wanted to savor every moment of freedom before heading to the academy for training.

"Ah! There you are—finally!" Zarmeena exclaimed, leaning against the railing that formed the boundary of the cemented platform where the cable car stopped for passengers. Frustration evident in her voice, she continued, "I almost gave up on you!"

"Sorry, sorry," Gul panted as she walked her bike towards the platform signaling the cable car operator to let them in. "Sorry, Zarmeena, you know Ma and Baa are leaving for Balakot, and as Palwasha wasn't home, I had to help them pack."

With a loud clang, the doors to the cable car slid open. Both girls lifted their bikes and settled themselves on the benches inside.

"Here, I made some sandwiches for us," Zarmeena offered, holding open a brightly colored picnic basket for Gul.

"Gosh! Thanks, Zarmeena, but let's wait until we reach the top," Gul replied.

"All settled in?" the young boy asked, handing them their tickets and checking the locks on the door.

"Yes we are!" Both girls nodded excitedly, taking the tickets and pocketing them carefully. "Thank you," she said, smiling and giving the boy a thumbs-up.

The cable car operator, seated in a glass-walled cabin, waved back. With a slight jerk and another loud clang, the cable car began its slow ascent. The weather being clear, the girls thoroughly enjoyed the view. The beauty of the valley never failed to amaze them, no matter how many times they took the ride. The emerald-blue lake dazzled like a giant gemstone at the heart of the valley.

"Can you believe how much beauty we're blessed with?" Zarmeena remarked, gazing at the still blue water below and enjoying the sunshine.

"Yeah!" Gul replied, squinting her eyes in the brilliant sunshine. "It's like these cable cars have given us wings." Gul enjoyed the fresh weather.

The cable car came to a stop with a loud clang. The girls, carrying their bicycles, got off, trying to keep their balance as they headed towards the bike trail. As they stepped out of the cable car, the cool mountain air greeted them. Gul and Zarmeena secured their bikes and adjusted their helmets, ready for their day of adventure. They could already hear the chirping of birds and the rustling of leaves in the gentle breeze.

"Let's try the new trail down that way," Gul said, pointing in the direction of a much wider path. "I will race you, Zarmeena!" Gul shouted, laughing. Both girls rode down the new path, feeling the fresh air on their faces. After a mile, they came to a small bend in the trail and slowed down. Finally, they got off their bikes as the curve was sharp and the dirt quite steep.

"Phew, that was fun!" Zarmeena shouted, out of breath. Feeling exhilarated, Gul nodded ecstatically, her face flushed with happiness.

"Wow! Yes, definitely it was amazing!"

As the girls trekked along the hill, feeling contented, they stumbled upon a lovely picnic spot. "Let's take a break here, I'm starving," Zarmeena suggested, suddenly feeling hot and hungry.

The two girls took out the sandwiches and lemonade from their bicycle basket and settled down on the lush green patch. "These are really, really good, Zarmeena," Gul remarked as she took a mouthful of the delicious sandwich speaking with her mouth full.

"Thanks," replied her cousin. "I knew we'd get hungry after the bike ride, and it's almost lunchtime, so I made plenty of them." She glanced at the hamper.

Gul had brought two plastic glasses for the lemonade, which she quickly poured for both of them. The cool, refreshing drink after the bike ride felt heavenly. The girls lay down on the grass, dozing on and off, basking as the warm sun rays played on their faces.

Suddenly, they were rudely awakened by a loud horn and the screeching of tires on the gravel road. "What in the wide world was that?" Gul cried, jumping up.

It was so sudden and loud that the girls felt a sudden rush of adrenaline, their pulses racing. They caught a glimpse of the back of a black sedan going around the bend, leaving a trail of dust and a frightened herd of cattle behind it.

"Thank God nobody got hit! Did you see the way he was driving the car?" Zarmeena snapped, angrily pointing in the direction of the disappearing vehicle.

Shaken and angry, Gul nodded brushing off dried twigs and grass from her dress. "And where do you think he was going?" she asked. "I'm pretty sure there's a dead end in that direction."

"I know! But it looked like they knew where they were going," Zarmeena retorted.

"You know what, Zarmeena? We should go and have a look," Gul suggested with indignation. "It was so wrong the way that person was driving the car—anybody could have gotten hurt. *We* could have gotten hurt!"

Zarmeena cut her off. "And what will we do even if we find the car?" she questioned, knowing very well how stubborn Gul could get. "Oh, all right," Zarmeena relented, throwing up her arms in the air. "I guess we can go have a look."

After walking for nearly twenty minutes, they reached a clearing. The road had widened, and a grand bungalow came into view.

"Oh!" they exclaimed simultaneously, stopping short in their tracks. Both girls halted as they caught the sight of the beautifully designed structure. It seemed to blend seamlessly with the surrounding forest as if it were an integral part of it. The exterior boasted a combination of concrete and wooden elements, adorned with a roof garden. It wasn't merely situated in the forest—it was a part of it.

"What a beauty," was all she Zarmeena could utter, unable to contain her awe. The sight of such a magnificent structure nestled in the middle of the forest was beyond their imagination. Both girls stood transfixed, completely overwhelmed by the sheer architectural brilliance of the bungalow.

"I wish I had a house like that," Zarmeena sighed, her gaze still fixed on the remarkable sight. However, her excitement quickly turned to concern when she realized Gul wasn't by her side. Looking around, she panicked for a moment before spotting Gul standing near the fenced boundary.

"Gul! What are you doing? Let's go! Why are you standing here like this?" Zarmeena urged, afraid someone might see them.

"Shh."

Confusion etched on her face, Gul continued to stare intently, almost as if she was looking at her own reflection. Her heart skipped a beat, and she couldn't believe her eyes; it felt like her mind was playing tricks on her.

Only a few could tell them apart, primarily close family and friends. Gul, being three and a half minutes older than Palwasha, shared a striking resemblance with her sister. Both girls possessed captivating beauty, with alabaster skin and finely sculpted features. Their intelligent gray eyes were framed by thick, arched eyebrows. Both the girls were intelligent and friendly, their personalities diverged beyond their physical similarities. Gul exuded patience and a sense of calmness, while Palwasha tended to be direct and straightforward in her approach. However, at this moment, Gul's calmness seemed to have vanished entirely.

"No, my mind is playing tricks on me," she murmured, feeling rooted to the spot.

Meanwhile, the group of people standing on the bungalow's porch had ascended the four flights of steps leading to the front veranda. Two men dressed in khaki and T-shirts, sporting aviator glasses, emerged with some heavy equipment in hand. From what Gul could see in the shadows of the tall trees, there were piles of leather bags stacked together. The entire group had gathered on the veranda, presenting an unusual sight. Among them, a tall woman wearing glasses and a white pantsuit stood out as the one in charge. Eventually, she moved away from the group, signaling the end of some discussion. Turning to three girls standing apart, she motioned for them to follow. Their movements were slow and filled with unease. Soon, everyone vanished inside. Gul and Zarmeena stood frozen, unsure of what to do or how to make sense of the situation, when they were suddenly frightened by something moving swiftly in their direction.

"Aaaah!"

Both girls shrieked simultaneously as a black beast appeared from nowhere. The fence stood as their only barrier. Barking fiercely, the creature attempted to leap over the fence but failed due to its height. It continued to strain and growl.

"Oh my god!" Zarmeena stumbled backward, tripping over a loose rock. Gul quickly moved away from the fence and helped Zarmeena up. Grabbing their bikes, the girls hurriedly ran toward a nearby bush for cover, but the huge dog continued to bark its head off.

"Shadow! Shadow!" a voice called out, drawing closer to where the massive Alsatian dog remained on guard. The girls could hear the voice approaching, causing Zarmeena to scramble.

"Ssshh. Shhh," Gul whispered to Zarmeena, who was struggling to keep herself from screaming, scared that the huge beast might jump the fence and come after them. By that time, the dog had mellowed to a soft growl.

A hefty man with a paunch appeared, whistling, "Hey, hey, buddy, calm down," he patted the dog, putting it on a leash, as he looked up and down the trail curiously.

The trail was empty.

"You were after the rabbits again, weren't you, Shadow?" he laughed. "Better luck next time buddy. Come, Shadow, come. Let's go inside!"

Gul observed the retreating back of the hefty man as she peered around the bush they had used for cover.

I wonder if he's the owner of the house, she thought to herself. Glancing back at her cousin, she whispered, "Zarmeena, come. Let's go. They're going back." Scrambling up, they retrieved their bikes, and without exchanging a word, they swiftly cycled down the trail. This time, it felt like the slope was on their side; they flew to the end of the trail.

"Hey, Gul! Look out!" Zarmeena exclaimed. "I almost somersaulted over you!" Zarmeena shouted angrily and out of breath. "Why did you stop?" She got off her bike.

Gul wore a dazed expression on her face and remained silent. Zarmeena's anger was quickly superseded by concern. Tapping Gul's shoulder, she asked, "What's wrong, Gul? Are you okay?"

Gul's eyes locked onto Zarmeena's face. "What was that, Zarmeena?" She pointed anxiously in the direction of the trail, almost getting emotional.

Zarmeena looked back, half expecting to see a menacing creature or something out of the ordinary. However, the trail appeared empty and devoid of any strange sightings. Her voice trembled as she faced Gul again. "Gul, what's the matter? Why are you so upset?" Zarmeena tried to console Gul as best as she could.

Brushing away Zarmeena's hand, Gul hastily picked up her bike and pointed it toward the house. "I'm going back up there."

"No, Gul. Stop, please," Zarmeena pleaded, circling around the bike and gripping the handle. "Gul, don't be reckless! There's no point in going up there now. Let's wait for Palwasha to come home, and then we can decide what to do!"

For a brief moment, Gul seemed frozen, just like the trees surrounding them. "Zarmeena, tell me. What was she doing up there in that strange house?" She couldn't shake off the unsettling feeling growing in the pit of her stomach. "She said she was going to the construction site with the workers."

Zarmeena, equally puzzled, struggled to find the right words to console Gul. "Listen, Gul. Let's try to stay calm and go home. I'm sure there's an explanation," Zarmeena attempted to reassure her, though deep down, she knew that calming Gul would be no easy task.

As they noticed other hikers approaching from the trail, Gul composed herself. Zarmeena gently nudged her forward, guiding her down the old path. The only sounds that disrupted their silence were the rustling of leaves beneath their feet, but even that noise seemed muted by their own thoughts. Lost in their individual contemplations, Gul occasionally glanced back, hoping to catch a glimpse of the other hikers. However, they had already taken a different trail, disappearing into the dense thicket. With the afternoon sun casting long shadows and the majestic Himalayan range preparing for the sunset, the atmosphere grew more serene, but it did little to ease the turmoil in the girls' minds.

The girls arrived back home just as the sun was setting. Zarmeena had come to stay with Gul for a couple of days since both of their parents were visiting their uncle and aunt in Balakot.

"You know, I've noticed that Palwasha hasn't been herself lately. We haven't been talking like we used to," Gul said.

"Not talking to you?" Zarmeena inquired. "Did you two have a fight or something?"

By now, the girls were sitting on the easy chairs in the long veranda, the sound of the splashing water in the water fountain providing a familiar backdrop.

Zarmeena poured some *qahwa* as Gul replied, "No, it's not a fight. It's just that she used to share everything with me, and now, she's been distant."

"Hmm," Zarmeena pondered, "you might just be overthinking." She patted her cousin on the knee. "Maybe she's been keeping her distance because you've been busy with your exams."

Gul sighed, shaking her head, her brows furrowing. "I don't know, Zarmeena. Something feels off—she's been coming and going at odd hours, and that's unlike her. And even if she is busy at the workshop, she would at least share it with me."

Zarmeena nodded in agreement. "Now that you mention it, Gul, she *has* been spending a lot of time with that reporter. Just a couple of days ago, I saw them together with some other girls near the hotel by the post office." Zarmeena continued, taking a sip of the *qahwa*.

"Oh, really?" Gul commented. "And did you talk to her?" The thought of her sister hiding things from her made her uncomfortable.

"No, no I didn't approach them," Zarmeena interjected, wishing she had not mentioned this to Gul before talking to Palwasha herself.

The clock inside struck midnight.

"Wow, look at the time, and she's still not home yet." Her tone carrying a hint of sarcasm, Gul glanced at her wristwatch.

Zarmeena felt a tad uncomfortable. "I think you were right—maybe we should have gone to that house. Or on second thought, maybe we should—"

"Hello! Hello, ladies…having a late-night party?" The cheerful voice of Palwasha greeted them. Oblivious to the tension in the air, Palwasha smiled at the girls and continued in the same vein. "Gosh, what a day." She sighed contentedly and threw herself onto one of the easy chairs, stretching out her legs. "I brought some shish kebabs for you girls," she said, taking out a Styrofoam box from her backpack.

Gul and Zarmeena awkwardly stood there in silence.

Palwasha was clearly in high spirits, unaware of the awkward silence she was met with. "Let me get the plates for you two," she said, quickly picking up her bag and heading inside.

Zarmeena, having witnessed the sisters' showdown numerous times before, was mentally preparing herself to play the peacemaker as always But Gul suddenly pressed her fingers against her lips. Zarmeena glanced toward the door, anticipating Palwasha's arrival at any moment.

"What are you doing, Gul?" Zarmeena asked, her eyes darting between Gul and the door.

"Listen, Zarmeena," Gul said, pulling her cousin away from the door, "let's keep quiet about it. Don't let on that we saw her at the guest house, and don't ask any questions." Gul urged her cousin and quickly moved away from Zarmeena and settled herself on the steps of the veranda.

Puzzled, Zarmeena shook her head. "Are you sure?" she whispered, hurrying to sit next to her cousin.

Gul patted Zarmeena's hand. "Yes, I am. I just don't want to confront her right now. I want to gather more details," Gul explained, trying to think of ways to get more information.

"More details? How's that?" Zarmeena pressed when Palwasha walked in.

"Here you go, girls!" Palwasha had changed into more comfortable pajamas and held a large tray filled with shish kebab, naan, and mint chutney. "I know it's midnight, but you can't have these kebabs the next day. That would be a disservice to their taste," she chirped, handing out the plates to her sister and cousin. "So what have you two been up to?" Palwasha sat cross-legged on the easy chair, stirring honey into her *qahwa*.

Before Zarmeena had a chance to speak, Gul quickly interjected, "Oh, a nice lazy day, nothing special." Gul's voice was artificially cheerful. Zarmeena carried a sheepish look on her face, looking away. Palwasha noticed their peculiar behavior and squinted her eyes at them. "You two look funny, especially you, Zarmeena. Is everything okay?"

Gul forced a laugh, thumping Zarmeena on her back, still not letting her cousin put in a word. "Oh, yes, yes. We're just tired of doing *nothing!* Seriously, Palwasha, you should have come with us. We rode our bicycles on the trail in the forest."

Palwasha held her stomach, shaking her head. "I'm full. I've already had too much."

Zarmeena, sitting in a nearby chair with her feet resting on the table, listened quietly to Palwasha's chatter about the shish kebab. Moving forward, she cautiously asked, "So how was your day, Palwasha?" purposely avoiding any mention of Anoosha.

"Oh…it was busy and hectic. We got the machines installed and will be able to start working properly next week," Palwasha explained. She certainly looked satisfied and happy.

"Hmmm, I'm glad you had a constructive day, Palwasha," Gul added, marveling at her sister's calm and content demeanor.

Palwasha reclined in the easy chair, folding her hands behind her head, her eyes closed as if she had not a care in the world. With her eyes shut, she continued, "I'm really enjoying taking on the whole project by myself." Opening her eyes momentarily, she looked at Gul with a hint of apology. "Don't get me wrong. I would obviously love to have you involved. It's our brainchild, both of ours. I just didn't want to rush you because of your exams, but now I expect you'll be helping me out." She smiled and, with a deep breath, stood up. "Girls, it's really late for me. I think I'm going to hit the bed." Noticing that neither of them moved, she chuckled lightly. "Are you girls planning to pull an all-nighter?" And without waiting for a response, she gathered the plates, balanced her mug on top of them, and proceeded inside. "Good night!" she called out. "And make sure you guys lock up."

Zarmeena was tired and ready to go inside, but Gul remained sitting. Not wanting to leave her cousin alone, Zarmeena hesitated. "Gul, shall we go inside? It's getting a bit chilly out here." Without uttering a word, Gul nodded and got up to go inside. Letting out a sigh of relief, Zarmeena hastily flicked off the porch light, closing the door behind them as they ascended the stairs to their shared bedroom.

Palwasha was already in bed, meticulously brushing her thick, long hair. As Gul and Zarmeena entered the room, she commented, "You both look exhausted. It's a good thing you came inside." However, Gul seemed disinterested in idle conversation. Without a word, she made her way directly to the adjacent dressing room to change. Zarmeena busied herself retrieving the sleeping bag from under the bed and unzipped it, preparing to lay it out on the carpeted floor.

Observing Gul's behavior, Palwasha couldn't help but inquire, her gaze fixed on the closed dressing room door. "What's wrong with her? She doesn't seem like herself today. Did something happen or what?"

Zarmeena, who was preoccupied with making her sleeping arrangements as comfortable as possible, began fluffing her pillow. "I think she might be a bit worried about her exam results," Zarmeena responded softly, trying to offer a plausible explanation.

Palwasha remained silent and unconvinced. "I know her results are really important, but she seems really upset today. Anyway, good night, cousin. I'm really tired. Will talk about Gul tomorrow."

And within a couple of minutes, Palwasha was sound asleep.

After a while, the dressing room door creaked open, and Gul emerged, holding a jar of Vaseline. She had overheard Palwasha's remark, but she too opted to ignore it. With Zarmeena settled in her sleeping bag and Palwasha already in bed, Gul switched off the light and climbed into her own bed. Despite her exhaustion, her mind continued to race, trying to make sense of the events that had transpired earlier in the day.

One thought dominated her mind: *What in the world was she doing at the guesthouse? And why would she lie to us about it?*

In the quietness of the room, the only sound was the gentle breaths of the two girls. Lying in bed, illuminated by the moonlight streaming through the window, frustrated Gul began counting the stars trying to get some sleep but always lost count midway and started again, using the bright North Star as her reference point. She turned on her side, humming a tune in her mind.

It twinkles like a star...no. It twinkles like a jewel in the sky. Gul played this game, describing the star in greater detail to help herself fall asleep, when she suddenly sat up. The grittiness of sleep was gone from her eyes.

"The gems! I completely forgot about the gems—they're in my shirt pocket," she whispered to herself. Carefully pushing away the covers, she tiptoed to the dressing room, careful not to disturb her roommates. Zarmeena shifted in her sleeping bag, almost making Gul jump out of her skin. With bated breath, Gul waited for a few seconds, ensuring her cousin was truly sound asleep before making her way to the dressing area. In the dark of the room, she blindly patted down her shirt.

"Phew, there they are." She heaved a sigh of relief. Clutching the small packet, she tiptoed back to bed. She looked at her sister and cousin, who were both sound asleep, and opened her palm. A crumpled white paper unfolded itself, revealing gleaming red beauties. There were like three stars in her hand. They appeared genuine, but Gul couldn't understand why they had been hidden in an unsuspecting bush in the forest!

Earlier that day, while the girls were hiding behind the bush near the guesthouse, Gul had accidentally struck her hand against something hard during her stumble. Her eyes had been drawn to a plastic bag partially buried under the soil. Without much thought, she had instinctively pulled at the corner, unveiling the surprising contents inside. Three radiant rubies rested inside the unassuming plastic bag. Acting on impulse, she had quickly stashed them in her shirt pocket, her attention mainly focused on the dog and the mysterious man in the poncho.

Were the rubies deliberately left there, intended for retrieval at a later time, or were they accidentally dropped? Countless questions flooded Gul's mind, but no answers presented themselves. As she drifted off to sleep, she found herself dreaming of fierce dogs with eyes gleaming like rubies, chasing her relentlessly through the jungle, while she ran tirelessly.

CHAPTER 7

The Workshop

"Anoosha's late...but she's never late!" said Palwasha agitatedly. It felt like the hundredth time she had looked at her watch. Suddenly, the door opened, and a face peered through. It was Zerka.

"Palwasha, the van is open, and we are unloading the material. Do you want to have a look? And also, Anoosha, ma'am is here asking for you!"

"Oh, good, finally," said Palwasha as she got up from her seat. "Tell Anoosha that I'm coming...no, wait! On second thought, don't tell her. Just organize the materials by color in the storage room. You don't need to say anything to her. I'll be out there in a minute."

Zerka, who was about to leave, stopped and turned back to say something. "Uhh...Palwasha"—the girl hesitated a bit—"I wanted to ask what happened to the paycheck? What should I tell the workers? What will they tell their families?" Zerka was the girl who was managing the accounts—and the pay date was already past due.

"Thank you, Zerka, for the reminder. Just tell the workers that they will be paid today, and sorry for the delay."

Zerka flashed a sweet smile. "Thank you, Palwasha. That's a load off my mind." And with that, she stepped out, closing the door behind her.

The small cabin served as an office space for the sisters; it was a small area cordoned off in the workshop. It was Palwasha's idea to have all the women working under one roof just like they did in the cottage industry. They were being supervised by the sisters and their cousin Zarmeena. Although Gul usually helped, lately she'd been preoccupied with her exams. On the other hand, Palwasha was the creative one. She was tasked with designing all aspects of the dresses from color combinations to cuts. Meanwhile, their cousin Zarmeena was the jack-of-all-trades, lending a hand in all aspects of the business. The workers were local ladies, excited to be able to work and also contribute largely to the community.

Business had already begun at the workshop, and their first target was to showcase their products at a renowned polo exhibition scheduled to take place in three weeks' time. Palwasha and Anoosha had been coordinating with the local authorities responsible for organizing the polo match. After numerous back-and-forth communications, they were now one step closer to achieving entrepreneurial success—they had secured permission to display their clothes during the opening ceremony. The Ministry of Arts and Culture was also dedicated to promoting local artisanal products to an international audience. In line with this objective, the ministry had allocated a certain amount of funding to various businesses to kick-start their operations. The ladies had also received this grant, but they needed to maintain a certain level of financial sustainability to ensure the continuity of their business operations. With all these obstacles, Palwasha and Anoosha had devised a plan—but they needed the right opportunity to execute it without anyone else knowing.

Palwasha picked up her bag and ventured into the main area of the workshop where boxes had already been unloaded. Gul and Zarmeena were overseeing the unpacking of the cartons while simultaneously assigning tasks to the female employees. There was an atmosphere of anticipation, and the entire place buzzed with the sound of sewing and cutting machines, reflecting the excitement felt by the businesswomen before the show. Palwasha made a brief stop at the nearest workstation, where a roll of powder-blue silk rested on the work counter. She ran her fingers across the material, reveling in its smooth and cool texture.

"Well, here you finally are," Gul greeted Palwasha with a wry smile as she approached her sister. She revealed a receipt to Palwasha, waving it in front of her face. "We got a big discount on the material," she said excitedly.

Palwasha heaved a sigh of relief and nodded. "Considering the quality of the silk, it's a miracle that we got any sort of discount." Not believing her luck, she took the receipt from Gul's hand and quickly scanned it to reassure herself. "Thank you. Because of you, we got this bargain, but we're not done yet." She looked at the small group. "We still need the threads to embroider our collection, and Anoosha has once again connected us with one of her countless contacts. Isn't that right, Anoosha?" Palwasha felt blessed to have found such a good and sincere friend in Anoosha.

Anoosha blushed, almost embarrassed. "I'll do as much as I can to help. You girls are an inspiration to all of us!"

Looking around the spacious hall, Palwasha remarked, "I just wish we had another cutting machine. It would have made things much easier for the workers, and they wouldn't have been so rushed. We need time to create a quality product."

Anoosha saw the opportunity and quickly chimed in, her voice filled with enthusiasm, "Yes, yes, that's why I talked to one of my friends. They might be able to help us!" She glanced at Palwasha. "That's why I want Palwasha to come with me."

CHAPTER 8

The Guesthouse

The work inside was now complete. When the girls had first visited the building, it still required finishing touches, but now it stood grand and beautiful. The lobby stretched out as a vast and open space, nearly square in shape, adorned with large French windows on either side. The windows allowed for natural light to pour in, creating a seamless connection between the indoors and outdoors.

"Wow! This looks truly stunning," Palwasha exclaimed, her gaze directed upward. "It feels like I've stepped inside a beautiful dome." The sunlit roof set the stage for a radiant beam of light that bathed the entire room. The front desk boasted a magnificent wall mural, giving the lobby a distinctive charm infused with the essence of the local culture. The ambience exuded a sense of peace and tranquility, creating a serene atmosphere. Anoosha, holding on to her bag with twinkling eyes, stared in sheer excitement. Her gaze shifted downward toward the man at the front desk, who seemed dwarfed by the mural behind him.

"Is the team for the photoshoot here yet?" she inquired, presenting her business card to the man.

"Yes, ma'am, they are here. However, I would kindly request you to wait in the waiting room for a few minutes," he quickly replied and led them to a small, secluded room that stood in stark contrast to the elaborate decor found elsewhere. "If you need anything, feel free to ring the bell on the table. I'll be right there," the receptionist politely said, pointing to a golden-colored dome star handbell placed on the center table. Anoosha nudged Palwasha into the coffee room, which was tastefully decorated with numerous lounge chairs and an array of pink accents. The focal point of the room was a huge mirror made of oak, finished in a rich mahogany brown. The light coming from the glass door of the lobby gave a sparkle to the room. Dumping her purse on the coffee table, Anoosha could sense Palwasha was getting a bit irritated.

"Let's wait here for a while," Anoosha suggested, gesturing toward the comfortable chairs. Looking restless, Palwasha ignored the suggestion.

Anoosha, noticing her friend's unease went up to her, "What's the matter, Palwasha? You need to relax."

Palwasha seemed a little dazed as she looked at Anoosha. "Anoosha, aren't you anxious as well? You know we lied to Gul about going for the funds, and now we're here at this guesthouse. There's no sign of the team in charge of the photoshoot, we're stuck in this stupid room, and it feels like we're just wasting time here. Do you think they canceled the shoot without telling us?"

"No, no, no. Why would you say that, Palwasha?" Anoosha tried to comfort her friend. "There's some meeting going on in the banquet hall with city officials. At least that's what the receptionist told me," Anoosha said, trying to console her friend. Palwasha was now pacing up and down the small room, tripping on her own feet.

"They gave me a specific time! What will I do if it gets late and Gul asks us about it and she's already behaving strangely toward me and I'm tired of lying to her and coming up with lame excuses?" she said, almost out of breath.

Realizing this was far from their ideal photoshoot, Anoosha gently grabbed her friend's shoulder. "You seriously need to calm down, Palwasha. Sit down and take a breather. Everything is going to be fine, and don't worry about your sister. What you're doing is for the workshop and the women working there—that's it!"

Palwasha took a deep breath, trying to think logically.

Anoosha continued, "It's only been a few minutes since we've been here. Worrying won't solve anything, and you of all people know that."

Palwasha looked at her friend, concerned. "You know, Anoosha, Gul didn't ask me anything when we left the workshop. I feel like she knows something is up."

"So? What can she do?" asked Anoosha, trying to find a solution.

"I don't know…I'm feeling uneasy about this whole situation," Palwasha said, feeling miserable.

Shaking her head, Anoosha stood up. "You've got your clothes for the photoshoot, right?" She was determined to shift the focus of the conversation. Palwasha simply patted her duffel bag, still looking dismayed. "At least we have something going for us," Anoosha said, trying to offer some reassurance. "You know what? You should start changing. Go into the powder room behind you. Come on, get up." After Palwasha failed to respond, Anoosha playfully grabbed her friend's arm in one hand and took the duffel bag with the clothes in the other. "Here. Go and change." Reluctantly, Palwasha took the bag, feeling somewhat deflated.

Anoosha heaved a sigh of relief. Glancing at her watch, she realized it had already been thirty minutes since they were shown the room. She muttered under her breath, "Once she's done changing, we're going to the banquet hall. Whether there are officials or not, it doesn't matter." Finally, after a few minutes, the door swung open, revealing a regal figure adorned with a long white *kamis* intricately embroidered with soft hues of pink and blue silk threads.

Anoosha couldn't help but exclaim, "Wow! You and the dress look absolutely beautiful!"

Palwasha accepted the compliment with a renewed sense of confidence. "This is our first sample piece," Palwasha said, gently running her fingers along the motifs adorning the neckline of the dress.

"The girls truly did an amazing job," Anoosha acknowledged, appreciating the craftsmanship.

"I guess I can do my hair as well while we're still waiting," Palwasha suggested, rummaging through her purse to find a hairbrush.

"Yeah, you should go do that," Anoosha agreed, poking her head outside the room through the opening of the door. "Actually, by the time you finish, we may be in luck. I just saw a group of men leaving the banquet hall. And I can do your makeup—that is, of course, if you allow me to," Anoosha said eagerly, searching for the vanity box Palwasha had taken out a couple of minutes ago. Both the girls stood in front of the small mirror, and Anoosha began braiding Palwasha's hair into a free-flowing sea of black.

Palwasha looked through the mirror and saw the last of the men leaving the banquet room. "I think the meeting is over now."

The man engaged in conversation with the guesthouse manager stood out vividly against the backdrop of the two girls' observation. Clad in a sleek dark suit, his presence was accentuated by the intense ripples of his attire. "We've taken every precaution to reserve a dedicated room for the photoshoot," the manager earnestly affirmed, breaking through the muffled ambience. "Rest assured, we'll have everything well in hand and neatly wrapped up before the chief guest arrives."

"Thank you so, so much," said the man, shaking hands with the manager. After bidding a curt farewell, they parted ways. The man in the suit remained in front of the coffee table, engrossed in texting someone, until a series of loud knocks on the glass door caught his attention.

The receptionist was talking to someone through the coffee room door, "Ma'am, they're all ready for the shoot," the man informed someone.

A shiver ran down the spine of the man in the gray suit. He was stunned by something that had caught his eye, standing motionless. It was the face: those thick, dark arched eyebrows and that dimple in the cheek.

Is it a figment of my imagination? he thought. To his annoyance, the reflection suddenly vanished just as it had appeared. His curiosity was piqued as he also heard a second voice that seemed distinctively familiar. Racking his brain, he tried giving a face to the familiar voice. He felt confused and frustrated.

What is going on?

On a sudden impulse, he wanted to go after the two girls down the hall but then thought better of it. *No...I should not act in haste,* he told himself. By now, the commotion behind him had stopped. Turning ever so slightly, he noticed that the hallway was empty. A bit dazed, he approached the receptionist and asked, "Excuse me... would you mind telling me what all that was about?" He pointed in the direction of the coffee room.

The receptionist nodded and smiled. "Yes, sir. They're the same group of people here for Ms. Farah's magazine shoot," the receptionist explained.

"I see..." he muttered, a thoughtful expression on his face.

"Is everything okay, sir?" The receptionist noticed the look on the man's face. "Would you like me to get you anything?"

"Oh no, no...I'm fine," the man in the gray suit assured him, giving a quick smile. "Thank you for all your help." With that, he turned around and walked out of the building and headed toward a black sedan waiting for him.

In the meantime, Palwasha and Anoosha hurried down the hallway into the banquet hall, where the cameras and lights were being set up, along with a navy-blue backdrop. As soon as the girls entered the hall, they were greeted by a shrill voice.

"Ah, there you are!" The voice belonged to a lady in her mid-thirties, dressed as if she was going to a costume party. The girls smiled at her as she rushed up to them, giving a quick peck on Palwasha and Anoosh's cheeks. "Come, come," she gushed, guiding Palwasha to a chair in a corner where a makeup table was laden with cosmetics and accessories. "Let me have a look." She picked up a moisturizer from the table and examined Palwasha's face in the mirror. "But oh, I did not notice. You've already done your makeup," she said, a bit taken aback.

"Thanks to her," Palwasha said, giving her friend a smile. "We were just trying to save everyone some time."

Anoosha nodded in agreement. "But if you think it won't work for the shoot, then go ahead you can add the final touches," Anoosha offered.

"No, no, it's good," the makeup artist cut her off, waving her hand. She smiled and reassured them, "We're mainly focusing on the jewelry, so no worries...I will tie up your hair in a bun since you have already braided it," she continued, gently fingering Palwasha's braided hair. Palwasha heaved a sigh of relief and settled back into the chair, allowing the lady to take over the rest of the work. Meanwhile, Anoosha had briefly stepped out. When she returned, Palwasha glanced at her watch, looking a tad bit annoyed. "Where are the rest of the girls? They're still not here," she asked, her gaze shifting to the makeup artist. "We are already late for the shoot!"

"Oh, they've already left," the lady replied without missing a beat, her focus remaining on styling Palwasha's hair.

"Left?" Palwasha countered. "But where to?" Confused, Palwasha looked at Anoosha, but before the makeup artist could answer, a singsong voice interrupted the conversation.

"There's my girl! And looking lovely as ever!" The woman, dressed in a beige pantsuit, briskly walked toward them. Her mouth was large, and the dark glasses perched on her small upturned nose added to her stylish appearance. She was a tall, attractive woman with a pleasant personality. "All ready?" she cooed, glancing around. "Come. Let's not waste any more time."

"Yes, Farah, we are all ready." Anoosha addressed the woman by name.

Farah was the CEO of one of the top labels in the country and also the co-owner of the guest house in Kunar Valley. Anoosha was on good terms with Farah and had done a lot of freelance work for Farah's label. And Anoosha was the one who had introduced Palwasha to Farah. It was common knowledge in the Valley that Palwasha, with the help of her father, had set up a small workshop, where they were manufacturing local handicrafts and clothing. With time, the workload and orders had started coming in, and as they were also showcasing their handicrafts at the exhibition during the polo festival, they were in need of finances. After meeting Palwasha, Anoosha had realized how passionate her friend was for the local ladies trying to become financially independent. Despite belonging to a relatively conservative family, Palwasha, along with three other girls from college, had agreed to do photoshoots for Farah's designer jewelry for a fashion and lifestyle magazine targeting international clientele. Palwasha was grateful to both Anoosha and Farah. Today marked the third round of their photoshoot, but the absence of the three girls was still bothering Palwasha. As the makeup artist retouched her makeup, Farah approached holding a blue velvet box in her hands.

"Here, put this on," Farah said, opening the box and revealing a stunning necklace. She carefully placed it around Palwasha's neck, the red gems glistening beautifully in the pale light.

"These are gorgeous," Palwasha remarked, touching the stones. "Are they real?" She was mesmerized by the rich red beauty of the gems.

Farah observed Palwasha with a knowing look. "No, dear, they're just imitations. But they look stunning on you," she replied, a faint smirk playing on her lips. Just then, the photographer called out to the crew, signaling the girls to step forward.

"We're all set! Bring the model to the front!" he shouted. Palwasha glanced at Farah, who nodded in approval, stepping back to allow Palwasha to take her place in front of the camera. The room filled with the sound of flashing lights. The photographer, a young and ambitious artist, directed Palwasha with fervor, clicking away at a rapid pace, just stopping a few times for Palwasha to change into different looks. The entire photoshoot lasted for almost three hours. Palwasha, who was tired and hungry, headed straight for the restroom to change.

Where is my bag? she asked herself, looking around. She remembered vividly that she had put it on the counter. Exhausted and feeling a bit agitated, she checked the bathroom stalls and the changing room, but it seemed to have vanished in thin air. Worried, she went back to the banquet hall.

"Excuse me," Palwasha approached one of the crew members, "I seem to have misplaced my bag. I had left it on the counter, but now it's gone. Have you seen it?"

The crew member, a young woman with a clipboard in hand, looked at Palwasha with a concerned expression. "I'm sorry, I haven't seen any bags around here. Did you check the lost and found? It's usually at the reception."

Palwasha's frustration grew. She felt a sinking feeling in her stomach. "No, I haven't checked there yet. I'll go and see if it's there. Thank you." She hurried to the reception area, her mind racing. Her bag contained her personal belongings, including her wallet and phone. She couldn't afford to lose them, especially in an unfamiliar place. At the reception, Palwasha approached the same receptionist who had shown them to the room earlier. "Excuse me," she said, trying to keep her voice calm. "I left my bag in the restroom near the banquet hall, but now it's gone. Have you come across it?"

The receptionist frowned. "I'm sorry to hear that. We'll do our best to help you find it. Let me check the lost and found for you." He stepped away momentarily to search through the items in the designated area.

Palwasha anxiously waited.

As the receptionist returned, Palwasha's eyes scanned the reception area, but her bag was nowhere in sight. "I'm sorry, ma'am, but we don't have your bag here," the receptionist informed her. "However, we can take your contact information and notify you if it turns up later. Sometimes things get misplaced and reappear later."

After giving her contact number, she left the reception and hurried back to the coffee room. *How could my bag disappear so suddenly?*

Meanwhile in the room, Anoosha sat on a chair, enjoying a cup of tea, until she noticed Palwasha searching for something. "What's the matter, Palwasha? What are you looking for?" Anoosha inquired, putting her teacup back on the coffee table.

Palwasha glanced at her friend and replied, "I can't seem to find my duffel bag!" She threw her arms up in frustration. "I've checked everywhere. It's not in the restroom or the changing room."

Anoosha pointed toward a gray duffel bag sitting on top of a coffee table near the restroom. "Isn't that the bag you're looking for?" she asked.

Bemused, she held her change of clothes in her hands. "That's strange. I'm pretty sure I took it with me to the restroom," Palwasha murmured, her brow furrowing in confusion. She unzipped her bag and carefully packed the clothes inside, hoping to find some clarity.

Anoosha observed her friend. "Hope you're not missing anything from your bag," she inquired, her voice laced with worry.

Palwasha shook her head reassuringly. "No, all the clothes are in here and my wallet." A warm smile graced her face as she closed the bag.

"Well then, let's continue, shall we?" Anoosha suggested, tucking away her half-finished cup of tea. She reached into her pocket and pulled out an envelope, its surface pristine and professional. With a genuine smile, she handed it to her friend, the recipient's name neatly typed in bold letters on the front. "And here is the paycheck for today's shoot," Anoosha announced, her voice filled with pride and satisfaction.

Palwasha gratefully accepted the envelope, a sigh of relief escaping her lips. "Thanks a lot, Anoosha. That's a weight off my shoulders. Now I can pay the workers and even buy some more materials!" Overwhelmed with gratitude, she pulled her friend into a tight bear hug, feeling a surge of warmth and appreciation.

Anoosha chuckled, reciprocating the embrace while holding onto Palwasha's hand. "Oh, come on now, what are friends for? There's no need to thank me. It's your hard work and dedication to a good cause, and I'm just glad to be a small part of it."

As the girls gathered their belongings, Palwasha glanced at her watch, raising an eyebrow in surprise. "Well, it's going to be a long night. Gul is going to be really mad at me. I'm sure of that," Palwasha exclaimed, a hint of worry tugging at her voice. "Come on, we need to start heading out."

As the girls made their way home, Palwasha felt a sense of satisfaction after a successful day of shooting. However, a lingering thought continued to nag at her. "Where were the other two girls?" she blurted.

Anoosha, keeping her focus on the road to navigate the hairpin turns, turned to her friend with a puzzled expression. "What do you mean?" she responded.

"The girls, Anoosha! They were supposed to be there for the shoot!" Palwasha suddenly turned in her seat, facing her friend in frustration. Her voice quivered with disappointment. "And remember, the makeup artist mentioned that they left? But they should have at least let me know. They had promised to give fifty percent of what they earned from the photoshoot!"

Anoosha listened attentively, empathizing with her friend's predicament. "Hmm…I agree, dear. They shouldn't have bailed on you like that." She sighed softly. "You know, I wanted to ask Farah about the girls, but she left before I could even talk to her." Pausing for a moment, she glanced at Palwasha, her expression thoughtful. "You did mention that you knew one of the girls from college. Why don't you try calling or texting her?" Anoosha suggested, turning into the driveway of Palwasha's house.

As the white Beetle approached the driveway, the black sedan that had been tailing it gradually slowed down. The man in the gray suit leaned forward, giving a signal to the driver to halt their progress. Anoosha, glancing at the rearview mirror, noticed the car behind them and grew concerned. "Did you see that car…the one that was following us?" she asked, her voice tinged with worry. Palwasha, who had been engrossed in texting one of the girls from their group, looked up with a puzzled expression.

"Uh…what car? Is someone actually following us?" Palwasha inquired, turning her head to look back, her eyes scanning the road behind them.

"The black sedan, Palwasha. It was tailing us all the way from the guest house," Anoosha revealed as she leaned out the car window, straining her neck to catch a glimpse of the vehicle. But to her surprise, there was no sign of the car. Palwasha, also taken aback by Anoosha's concern, looked around but found no trace of the mysterious car. She brushed off the situation with a lighthearted tone.

"Oh, come on, Anoosha! Why would anyone want to follow the two of us? It's not like we're smuggling anything!" With a playful gesture, she gave a friendly smack on Anoosha's back, winking mischievously. "But on second thought, my sister might have hired a private investigator to keep an eye on us," Palwasha speculated, amused.

They giggled, and Anoosha felt a sense of relief wash over her.

"Hmmm," Anoosha murmured, observing Palwasha as she attempted to call the girl again. However, there was still no response, and Palwasha waved her mobile phone in front of Anoosha with frustration.

"Why do people even have phones if they never answer? I've tried five times!" she wailed.

As the girls descended the steps that led to the front veranda, the evening sun started to dip below the horizon, painting the sky with hues of fiery orange and dark purple. The breathtaking beauty of the dusky sky, however, went unnoticed by the girls as they remained lost in their own thoughts.

CHAPTER 9

Back Home

The veranda's lights emitted a dull yellow glow, casting a warm ambiance. The main door stood open, allowing muted voices of conversation to drift through the screen door. Palwasha stepped inside, followed closely by Anoosha, who would be staying with the sisters and their cousin until the day of the polo match. As they entered, the tantalizing aroma of dinner being prepared enveloped them, igniting their appetites.

"There you are, just in time for dinner!" Gul greeted them, her smile radiating warmth. Both Gul and Zarmeena were busy setting the table and serving the meal.

"Oh, *biryani*! How lovely! I'm absolutely famished. In fact, we're both quite hungry," Palwasha exclaimed, her eyes gleaming with anticipation. She inhaled deeply, sniffing the air like a happy pup. Zarmeena joined in, assisting with the cutlery and carefully filling the glasses with water.

As Anoosha surveyed the beautifully set table, a genuine sense of gratitude shone in her eyes. "This looks and smells amazing," she remarked. "Thank you all for letting me stay with you." With a grateful smile, she took the first bite of the delectably spiced rice.

"Oh, Anoosha, don't be so formal," Gul responded, her tone friendly. "You're always welcome here. You've been a great help to *most* of us." There was a subtle hint of sarcasm in Gul's tone. However, Anoosha, engrossed in savoring the delicious food, didn't seem to notice the underlying tension and continued enjoying her meal.

"Gul and Zarmeena, you guys have truly outdone yourselves. This is incredibly yummy," Palwasha complimented, her taste buds dancing with delight.

Before Gul could respond, Zarmeena interjected, her expression serious as she looked directly at Anoosha. "Oh, this is my aunt's recipe, and it always turns out great," she stated matter-of-factly. With that remark, the rest of the meal continued in silence, punctuated only by the occasional clinking of cutlery. Gul seemed uninterested in engaging in casual conversation with either her sister or Anoosha, while Palwasha found herself lost in her own thoughts. She pondered the unanswered phone calls, Gul's peculiar behavior, and the underlying tension in the air. The day seemed to be ending on an oddly uncomfortable note.

What a strange end to the day, Palwasha mused to herself, a hint of confusion lingering in her thoughts.

After clearing up the table and washing the dishes, the four girls ascended the stairs. Palwasha led her friend to the guestroom, conveniently located next to the girls' room. The room had a simple yet comfortable design, featuring a queen-sized wrought-iron bed and a captivating painting of snow-capped mountains hanging above the headboard.

Anoosha approached the bed, gazing at the artwork. "Wow, is this yours?" she inquired, leaning closer to examine the signature at the bottom of the painting.

Palwasha beamed with pride, her eyes sparkling. "Oh, that's my mom's…she's the one who painted it," she replied, her voice brimming with pride for her mother's artistic talent.

Anoosha's admiration was evident as she commented, "What a gem of a family you lot are!" She then expressed her gratitude, placing her bag on the dresser. "Thank you once again for your warm hospitality, Palwasha. You have a great family." She hugged her friend.

Palwasha responded with a genuine smile. "Hospitality is ingrained in the people of our valley, and we're always here to help. If you need anything, don't hesitate to ask. We're just next door. Good night, dear, and thank *you*!"

CHAPTER 10

Najeeb's Tip

"Sir, shall we proceed to the assistant commissioner's house?" the driver of the black sedan inquired as they drove past the parking lot. Ever since they had departed from the guesthouse, the man in the gray suit had maintained an unusually quiet demeanor. The sole instruction he had given was to tail the white beetle.

"Yes, head to the AC house," the man ordered firmly. As they descended the winding mountain road, Najeeb's mind was consumed with deep contemplation. What he'd seen at the guest house had left him bewildered and perhaps even a tad angry.

I need to have a conversation with them, but who should I approach? Who was there? Gul or Palwasha? A cascade of questions flooded his mind until a sudden realization dawned upon him. *"The reflection! It was the reflection and the dimple... It was on the right side instead of the left... It was Palwasha at the guesthouse!*

"Sir, we have arrived," the driver's voice interrupted Najeeb's train of thought. He looked up and noticed that the driver had already opened the door, waiting patiently for him. Najeeb bid the driver good night and stepped out of the car. He was staying at the government guest house as he had come to the valley to oversee the preparations for the upcoming polo tournament, which would be attended by several foreign dignitaries. Najeeb's personal orderly was waiting inside to serve him dinner, but at that moment, Najeeb had no appetite. He was weary and agitated, longing for nothing more than a steaming cup of coffee and the comfort of his study to ponder over the events that had unfolded earlier that evening. The orderly noticed the fatigue etched on Najeeb's face and realized that he would prefer not to be disturbed. However, he decided to take a chance.

"Sir, dinner is ready," he quietly told him.

Najeeb was about to reprimand him, but Aziz was his longtime personal aide, more like an elderly uncle. Despite having no appetite, he smiled at the man. "Please bring me something light to eat and a large mug of coffee…and thank you, Aziz, for everything." With that, he retreated to his study. Najeeb had freshened up and was going over one of his files when his cell phone rang, shattering the silence of the study. He picked up the phone, but the caller ID displayed as unknown. As he speculated about the caller's identity, the phone's battery died. Almost simultaneously, a soft knock on the door signaled Aziz's entrance, carrying a tray adorned with chicken sandwiches, fruit salad, and a steaming bowl of hot and sour soup. Surveying the delectable spread, he suddenly realized how hungry he was! Filling up his plate, Najeeb made himself comfortable in the big leather armchair, turning on the television to a news channel.

"Is there anything else you need, sir?" Aziz inquired, adding hurriedly. "I will be bringing your coffee shortly. Also, sir, there's an envelope for you. It was found near the rose bed by the gardener." Aziz explained, handing over a large manila envelope to Najeeb with his name neatly written in big bold letters on the front. Curious, Najeeb took the envelope and examined it.

"But there is no return address on it," he commented, scrutinizing the envelope from both sides, "and no stamp either. That's strange." He looked at Aziz. "Did the gardener see anyone who wasn't supposed to be on the grounds?"

Aziz shook his head. "No, sir. The gardener saw no one."

"Okay, thank you, Aziz. See you in the morning then." Najeeb dismissed his orderly, who gathered up the dirty plates and went out, carefully closing the door behind him. Suddenly, the phone rang again, but just as Najeeb was about to pick it up, it stopped.

He turned his attention back to the brown manila envelope when the phone rang again.

"Oh, come on!" He snatched the phone off the table in irritation before the caller could disconnect the call. "Hello...*hello?*" he repeated, but there was silence on the other end. "Hey, whoever it is, say something or don't waste my time calling!" Still, there was no reply, and he disconnected the call.

"Weird...the whole day has been weird," he muttered to himself. He got up and walked over to the coffee table, picking up the mysterious envelope and staring at it for a few seconds. He took a deep breath and carried it to the study table. Opening the drawer, he retrieved an envelope opener and carefully slid it under the flap to loosen it. Just as he was about to look inside, the sudden ping of a notification on his cell phone caught his attention. Still holding the opener, he swiped open his phone and accessed the message icon. Clicking on it, he saw a message from the same unknown number:

> Khalil and Baaz handling rubies...Peshawar...
> entering Chitral in a couple of days...white jeep
> AB 1223 Peshawar.

Najeeb felt a rush of adrenaline as he read and reread the message. Whoever sent this message must be someone quite close to these two characters, he thought to himself. Without thinking, he redialed the number from which he had received the message. The connection was being established, but there was no response. "Okay, you are not going to get away that easily," he remarked with determination in his voice. His pulse raced as he tried to recall the number, but this time, the cell was powered off. Najeeb stared at his cell phone, frustration building up inside him. He couldn't shake off the feeling that something was amiss. The mysterious envelope, the cryptic message, the unanswered calls—it all pointed to a puzzle he needed to unravel. Setting the phone aside, he turned his attention back to the envelope and finally opened it. Inside, he found a handwritten note on a plain sheet of paper. The writing was neat and precise, with each word carefully penned.

As he read the message, his eyes widened in disbelief:

> Khalil and Baaz handling rubies…Peshawar… entering Chitral in a couple of days. Jeep AB 1223 Peshawar.

He grabbed his phone and redialed the unknown number. This time, the bell started ringing. "Pick up…pick up!" Adrenaline rushed through Najeeb's body, and to his surprise, somebody declined the call. Najeeb's mind raced as he tried to make sense of it all. Najeeb turned back to the envelope and shook it, eager to uncover the rest of its contents. Two black-and-white photos emerged, their quality slightly grainy as if captured by a less sophisticated device. Examining the photos, Najeeb returned to his chair, fixating on one image in particular.

The man with the beard… Had he encountered him before?

Something about the man's face struck a chord within Najeeb. Perplexed, he continued to study the photo intently, realizing the urgency of arranging a meeting with the local law enforcement as soon as possible.

With a determined look on his face, Najeeb picked up his cell phone and dialed the number for DSP Chitral: The Deputy Superintendent of Police, who also happened to be his friend and course mate from the academy. The bell rang on the other end, and Najeeb glanced at his watch, noting that it was well past midnight.

Just as he was considering ending the call, a gruff voice on the other end answered with a sleepy "Hello."

Without wasting any time, Najeeb went straight to the point. "Ali, I know it's late, but this is very important."

The voice on the other end interrupted him. "Najeeb, is everything all right?" Ali's concern was evident in his tone. He was now wide awake.

"Yes, yes, all good. Listen, I just sent you a text. You need to look into it, and I will meet you in the morning as soon as I can."

Najeeb and Ali had been sharing information about an ongoing investigation, and nearly all internal security agencies were involved. Ali's somber voice came through.

"Yes, I received your text, Najeeb, and we can definitely have the meeting at my office tomorrow." Ali confirmed the time. "Is there anything else?"

Najeeb shook his head. "No, but we need to run a background check using the number plate. Can you assign your team to that?" Najeeb requested.

"No problem… Let's talk tomorrow. I'm hoping this isn't some prank and that the information is authentic. By the way, how did you obtain this info?" Najeeb shared the details of the phone call and the mysterious envelope with Ali.

"We'll have to track the number. It could be a significant lead," Najeeb stated. "Anyways, good night, and see you in the morning." With that, he ended the call.

Just as the day had been strange, the night proved to be restless for Najeeb. He tossed and turned in bed, attempting to find a cool spot under the covers, but he couldn't relax.

"Ughh," he groaned.

Pushing off his covers, he sat up and checked his watch. "It's only two thirty," he muttered, sitting at the edge of the bed. His shoulders were hunched, head down, his mind again to the morning events.

I need to straighten things out…and quickly. I have to speak to Gul too, he thought. *Should I ask her directly what Palwasha was doing at the guesthouse? If she says yes, then what? But it was Palwasha at the guesthouse—not Gul. So should I ask Palwasha and not Gul?*

Frustrated, Najeeb opened up the bedside drawer and took out a pack of cigarettes. The pack was untouched. Ripping off the cellophane packing, he took one out and put it in his mouth and looked for his lighter…but of course, there was none; Gul had taken it. In fact, she had almost snatched it from him in order to remind him how she hated for him to smoke. He just sat there, with the unlit cigarette dangling through his lips when the quiet of the night was shattered by the ringing of his phone, and as suddenly as it had started, the ringing stopped. Najeeb recognized the number and hastily grabbed his phone from the nightstand.

"*Gul?*"

It was a missed call from Gul. He dialed her number, feeling a surge of panic shooting through him. The screen showed "*Ringing.*"

"Why isn't she picking up?" he wondered out loud, waiting for her to answer the call.

"Hello?" came a wary voice.

"Hello, Gul? Are you okay?" Najeeb asked, feeling a bit relieved upon hearing her voice. "You called?"

Let her say whatever she wants to say herself, he thought.

"I'm sorry for calling you at this time, and yes…everything is fine." Najeeb could feel her hesitation. "I wanted to ask you if we could meet tomorrow?" She spoke in low, hushed tones.

"Gul, where are you?" Najeeb asked, puzzled by her demeanor.

"I'm at home, obviously," came the curt reply. "It's just that Palwasha and Zarmeena are sleeping, and Anoosha is also here with us," she whispered.

"Anoosha?" Najeeb couldn't place her, feeling a bit confused.

"Palwasha's reporter friend," she whispered impatiently. "Listen, can we meet tomorrow?" she insisted again.

"Yes, of course," Najeeb agreed. "I have a meeting in the morning, and I'm not sure how long it will take, but we can have lunch together." The minute the words escaped his mouth, he immediately regretted them, knowing fully well that Gul would object to the idea of them going out together.

"Okay, fine…where?" Her response was instant.

Najeeb raised his eyebrows, staring foolishly at the cigarette packet in the open drawer. He couldn't believe his ears. Keeping his tone normal, he said, "I'll pick you up from the workshop, and then we can have lunch wherever you want."

"All right. And thank you. Good night."

The line went dead, and Najeeb just sat there, phone in his hand, at a loss for words. "Well, this definitely takes the cake for all the weirdness and madness of the day."

CHAPTER 11

On Track

"Hello, Najeeb! Good to see you, buddy." Ali greeted his friend enthusiastically, giving him a bear hug. "Come, sit." He pointed to the leather chairs in the corner of the room.

Taking the seat, Najeeb came straight to the point. "Ali, any progress regarding the info I passed on?"

Ali nodded, smiling at his friend. "That info was good, and I had my people put an APB on the car. Earlier today, they got back to me. The car in question entered Balakot this morning, and we put a tail on the car." Ali paused and looked at Najeeb, who was sitting still with a worried expression on his face. "Najeeb, all this is quite sensitive. Where did you get the information from?" Ali was looking at his friend with concern. He moved forward in his chair. "Look, tell me what's going on?"

Najeeb nodded and recounted the whole episode of the manila envelope and the anonymous phone call, giving him the tip. "And here are the photos that were in the envelope," Najeeb continued, handing Ali the photos.

Ali studied the photos closely. "So these are the two men whose names were mentioned in the message?"

"That's right," Najeeb nodded, "but we don't know who is who and whether the names are real or just aliases."

"Right, right," Ali agreed. With a brooding look, he got up and went to his desk, dialing a number and putting the phone on speaker.

"Hello," someone on the other end of the line greeted him.

"Oh, yes, hello, Faraz. This is Ali. Anything more regarding the white jeep?"

The person on the other end informed him that the jeep was registered to a man named Karim Khan, living in Landikotal, a town just a few kilometers inside Pakistan from the Afghan border. "I am faxing you his ID, and as for the car itself, our men are on its tail, so whenever you want us to apprehend them, just give us a signal."

Ali looked at Najeeb for confirmation, but Najeeb shook his head.

"Okay, Faraz, good work, but right now, we just want to keep those in the jeep in sight. Tell your men not to lose their track and keep me posted for any new developments."

"Right, sir…and good day, sir," came the curt reply, and the phone went dead.

Ali turned to face his friend, his eyes shining with excitement. "Well, the game is on, my friend. Our very first tip regarding the vehicle number a few months back was correct. The smuggled stones will be exchanging hands here in this valley." Najeeb was a bit skeptical, not sharing Ali's enthusiasm, and it didn't go unnoticed by his friend. "What is bothering you, Najeeb? This is good news. After weeks of lull, we are finally seeing some movement, but you seem lost. What's on your mind?"

"The thing that's bothering me is that the information I received didn't come from any external source. It came from someone who lives here in this valley. Otherwise, why would anyone deliver an envelope by hand? That person knows me and my number."

Ali nodded thoughtfully. "That completely slipped my mind, and you're right. This hits close to home. Najeeb, do you want a security guard at your disposal? I'm concerned for your safety."

But Najeeb chuckled, smiling at Ali.

"No, buddy, I'm good. But put someone to track the cell number. This could certainly be the break we're looking for!"

Ali thumped Najeeb's back, grinning at his friend. "Don't worry, I'm on it." The rest of the morning passed with Najeeb and Ali engrossed in their respective departments, attending to their routine work.

CHAPTER 12

The Lost Rubies

Gul, after her conversation with Najeeb the previous night, placed the phone down and nestled back into her bed.

Is it the right decision to involve Najeeb in something I myself am uncertain about? she wondered.

Doubt began doubting her choice to confide in Najeeb. *And what about Palwasha? Should I confront her first?*

Turning on her side, she thumped the pillow in frustration, desperately trying to find a comfortable angle. However, sleep remained elusive. What hurt her the most was the fact that her own twin sister hadn't confided in her. Instead, Palwasha appeared more at ease with Anoosha, and that caused a deep pang of hurt. To make matters worse, Palwasha had intentionally lied to her. She thought wistfully, attempting to suppress the feelings of being ignored and the growing resentment toward Anoosha that gnawed at her. Throwing aside her covers, Gul sat up, folding her knees against her chest and wrapping her arms around her legs. She remained seated, attempting to sort out her feelings, when suddenly, she remembered the three glistening rubies she had discovered beneath the hydrangea bush in front of the guesthouse.

"The rubies!" she silently exclaimed. "I need to retrieve them now, otherwise tomorrow I may or may not have the opportunity to go to the barn." Gul had hidden the rubies in the barn, fearing that placing them inside the house would risk someone discovering them. She wanted to avoid any kind of confrontation, especially with Anoosha present. Gul intended to show the rubies to Najeeb and share everything she and Zarmeena had witnessed.

She took a deep breath and tiptoed out of her room toward the guestroom. The door was slightly ajar, and she could hear Anoosha snoring away.

Thank God she's not sharing the room. Otherwise, I wouldn't have slept a wink, Gul thought to herself, peering in at Anoosha. It was hard to imagine a delicate girl like her snoring so loudly; it was almost comical.

It's like a gigantic bumblebee that just discovered a black hole on a wild joyride and decided, "Hey, why not give it a whirl?" She laughed quietly and moved quickly away from the door, shaking her head.

What a peculiar analogy. I wish I could say it to her face. She chuckled under her breath, careful not to make any noise, and descended the stairs. In the mudroom downstairs, Gul silently slipped on her loafers and exited through the back door, closing it cautiously behind her. Jogging along the track toward the barn, she patted her pocket to ensure she had the key. "Gosh, this is nerve-wracking," she muttered, glancing around. "I wish the sky wasn't so cloudy today." Everything looked so dark and spooky. And as Gul looked back over her shoulder, she suddenly cried out in pain, "Ouch!" She had tripped over a loose stone.

"Uff, that was close. I should have brought my torch," she complained, flexing and extending her ankle to ease the pain and ensure there was no sprain. Suddenly, she stood still, her heart thumping loudly as she held her breath. She was sure she had heard something. Cautiously, she looked around, trying not to shake, but all was quiet except for the night sounds of crickets chirping and the distant howl of a wolf. Trying to calm her nerves, she took in a long breath and made a dash for the barn door, gripping the key tightly in her hand for reassurance. She crossed the steps in one long jump, her heart racing, and attempted to insert the key into the keyhole. However, her hands were shaking so much that the key wouldn't go in.

"This can't be happening," she panicked, startled by the howling of coyotes. In her fear, the key slipped from her fingers and fell to the floor.

"Oh no, where is it?" She hastily dropped to her knees and searched in the dark, her fingers gathering dust. Suddenly, a hard, cold object collided with the side of her left hand.

"Found it." She exhaled with relief, a wave of comfort washing over her. Sliding the key into the lock, she turned it swiftly, and the door opened with a slight creak. In one swift motion, she stepped inside and quickly locked the door. Now she stood in complete darkness, leaning against the door as she gathered her composure. Gradually, her eyes adjusted to the dim surroundings of the barn, where in the far-right corner of the room, she could just barely discern the dark rectangular shape of the telescope box. Moving with caution, she delicately flipped open the box and reached inside, her hand searching for the plastic bag containing the precious gems. As luck would have it, her hand landed directly on top of the bag. Carefully retrieving it, she tucked it away in her shirt pocket. Returning to the door, she opened it cautiously, peering outside to ensure no one was around. Satisfied that the coast was clear, she wasted no time and swiftly locked the door behind her. Without casting a second glance, she sprinted all the way home, yearning for the safety and comfort of her bed. Upon arriving home, she silently slipped through the back door and secured the lock. With utmost stealth, she ascended the stairs. Pausing momentarily on the landing, she listened intently, ensuring that no one was awake. The only sound that reached her ears was Anoosha's gentle snoring.

"The bumblebee is still busy," Gul muttered under her breath, her words barely audible. Moving away from the door, she proceeded down the hallway toward her bedroom. Standing outside, she paused, assessing whether both her sister and cousin were still sound asleep. The last thing she wanted was to face their barrage of curious questions at this hour. Listening intently, she was greeted by nothing but silence. With caution, she slowly turned the doorknob and entered the room, treading softly on tiptoes. Her cousin lay in her usual manner, resembling a matchstick in a box—straight and mouth slightly ajar. Glancing over at her sister, she found her curled up in a fetal position, sound asleep like a contented baby. Gul approached her sister's side of the bed with utmost care, gingerly removing the two pillows she had strategically placed underneath the covers to create the illusion of her presence. Slipping under the covers herself, Gul released a sigh of relief, feeling the weight of the world lift off her shoulders.

CHAPTER 13

The Encounter

The weather was undeniably gloomy, casting a somber veil over the world outside. Thick gray clouds hung low in the sky, blocking out the sun's cheerful rays and replacing them with a pallid, diffused light. A fine mist of rain drizzled from the heavens, veiling the landscape in a damp shroud. The air was heavy with moisture, creating a chilly atmosphere. In contrast, the mood inside was totally the opposite.

Palwasha, who was on the phone with Zarka, walked in, and with an air of jubilation, she clapped her hands and shouted, grinning from ear to ear, "The Ministry for Art and Culture has approved more funds for us!" She hugged Gul, who was standing against the kitchen counter, smiling fondly at her sister.

"Palwasha, I am so happy for you. Your hard work, along with that of Zarmeena and the rest of the workers, has finally paid off." Gul beamed at Zarmeena and gave them a thumbs-up. "Baba would be so proud of you!"

Anoosha, who had been in the living room, joined the sisters and their cousin. The kitchen was filled with jubilation and happiness, creating a stark contrast to the weather outside. Excitement brimmed in the air as everyone spoke simultaneously, offering suggestions and making plans for the exhibition and their strategy to meet the deadline. Perched on the kitchen counter with a contented expression, Palwasha resembled a coach about to gather her team.

She let out a sharp whistle, causing the chatter to cease abruptly. Surprised gazes turned toward her.

"Who do you think you are, a referee?" Zarmeena asked playfully, her smile directed at her cousin. Palwasha cleared her throat as if preparing to deliver the most important speech of her life. She pointed solemnly at the stacked Styrofoam boxes on the kitchen table.

"Don't forget, we also need to pack lunch boxes for our workers."

Despite it being the weekend, the girls had decided to have the workers come in for overtime as the deadline was rapidly approaching. The workers had agreed, and in order to make the situation more enjoyable, the girls had taken on the task of preparing lunch for them. With breakfast finished, the table cleared, and the dishes washed, the sisters and their cousin gathered to make pilaf, a local specialty. Earlier that morning, Gul had soaked the rice, and now she was toasting the orzo, its earthy aroma permeating the entire kitchen. Sauteing the spices vigorously in the butter, Gul called out to her sister.

"Hey, Palwasha, could you please keep an eye on the vegetable broth? We don't want it to boil over."

Palwasha, who was busy sauteing the meat and humming one of her favorite songs, winked at her sister and said, "No worries! Your sous-chef is here, and I'm an expert at multitasking. It won't boil over—not on my watch!"

With a smile, she increased the flame to help the water evaporate quickly from the meat. Meanwhile, Anoosha returned to the kitchen after changing upstairs. She inhaled deeply, scrunching her nose.

"Wow! This smells amazing! What are you guys cooking?" She looked over Palwasha's shoulder. "Is it cooked?" Anoosha asked, taking a small piece of meat from the bone and popping it into her mouth. Instantly, she cringed, trying not to scream.

"Hey, watch it!" Palwasha warned, looking concerned. "You are going to burn yourself!" Anoosha did a juggling dance, her eyes watering as she rolled the piece of meat around in her mouth.

"Gosh! It's so hot, but it's so tender and juicy." Her face was blushing.

Gul chuckled, "Anoosha, we'll have it for dinner, don't worry. But for now, could you please help Zarmeena assemble the rice and meat in the lunch boxes?" Although Gul asked Anoosha politely for a favor, there was still a hint of derision in her tone, and everyone in the room felt it. Zarmeena glanced sideways at Gul, who had busied herself washing the pots. Palwasha too was taken aback by Gul's tone as it was unlike her sister to speak to someone like that, especially a guest. Palwasha wanted to retort but remained quiet, not wanting to create a scene in front of Anoosha. An awkward silence filled the room, and to break it, Anoosha chimed in, squeezing Palwasha's hand.

"Let's start making those lunch boxes!" She winked at her friend, trying to lighten the mood. The next half hour was spent packing the lunch boxes and stacking them in Anoosha and Gul's car. By eleven-thirty, the girls were on their way to the workshop, and by the time they arrived, it was almost lunchtime for the workers. They carried the lunch boxes to a shed next to the main building, which served as the makeshift dining and rest area for the workers. Inside the shed, there was a long wooden table with long wooden benches on either side. The girls placed the stacked lunch boxes and seven cartons of fresh lemonade at one end of the table. Gul and Palwasha had already entered the main building where work was in full swing. The workers were occupied at their workstations, while Zarka assisted a group of laborers at a cutting station, responsible for the men's long coats—one of the most challenging tasks that required the expertise of a skilled tailor.

Zarka saw Gul and Palwasha and waved at them excitedly. Hurriedly walking up to them, she said, "Hi, Gul. Hi, Palwasha! The amount the ministry sanctioned came through. I just got a call from the bank!" She shook hands with the sisters one by one.

Gul smiled and said, "That is such great news for both of you!" She looked at her sister and Zarka, adding, "It's a good omen for the days ahead. And Zarka, we have food in the shed, so please dismiss the workers for lunch." Nodding enthusiastically, Zarka blew the whistle hanging around her neck, signaling the noon-time break. The girls then got busy in the office. Palwasha was the brain behind designing the clothes, while Gul handled the accounts, with Zarmeena assisting both sisters whenever it was required. All three of them were engrossed in their work when Zarmeena's stomach growled so loudly that the girls burst out laughing.

"Gosh, I didn't know I'd be this hungry," Zarmeena muttered sheepishly. Gul put her pen down, pointing toward a picnic basket sitting in the corner of the room.

"There's chicken salad in there for all of us. You guys take a break. I just need to stretch my legs," Gul said, leaving the office. Out in the open, she could think more clearly; the lunch meeting with Najeeb was still on her mind, and she was questioning whether to confide in Najeeb first or confront Palwasha straight away. So engrossed in her train of thought, she didn't notice a blur of an Alto pulling up in the parking lot. It was only when the girl was standing right in front of her that she realized the girl was addressing her as Palwasha.

"Here, take this," the girl scowled, thrusting a bag into Gul's hands. "The dress is in the bag, and listen, Palwasha, do not bother me again. I am not interested in that stupid photo shoot." And without waiting for an answer, the strange girl turned on her four-inch heels, strutted back to her car, and was gone in a matter of minutes. Everything happened so fast that Gul didn't even get a chance to respond. For the first few minutes, she just stood there like a dummy, holding the bag in her hand and staring at the empty parking lot. Then it struck her that the girl obviously knew her sister and was talking about some photoshoot. Gul looked around to check if anybody was nearby, and seeing no one, she hastily opened the bag. To her surprise, the bag revealed a lilac dress. This was no ordinary dress, though. It was the same dress Palwasha had designed for the very first time and intended to showcase along with her other designs. Confused, Gul shoved the dress back into the bag.

What was this dress doing with that girl? And why did she mention a photo shoot?

Gul wanted answers, and for that, she would have to go to the guesthouse. Just as she made up her mind, her phone rang, snapping her out of her thoughts.

Oh, shucks, it's Najeeb.

She had completely forgotten about their meeting. *Should I ignore the call? I'll just text him. It'll save me from coming up with excuses.*

Because of what had happened just a few minutes ago, she didn't want to discuss anything with Najeeb or Palwasha. Just as the girl's words had implied, Gul assumed that the guest house was where the photo shoots were taking place, and she felt the need to investigate. Instead of returning to the workshop, she headed toward her car but soon realized that the car keys were still in the office. Frustrated, she texted Zarmeena, asking her to bring the keys outside without informing anyone, waiting patiently behind her car, concealed from anybody looking outside from the workshop. As she stood there, a drop of water landed on Gul's cheek, prompting her to look up and witness the rapid gathering of gray clouds, swiftly obscuring the once-blue sky.

"It's going to rain…and rain hard," she muttered, observing the ominous columns of clouds. Growing restless, she wondered what was taking Zarmeena so long. Just then, as if by magic, she heard a tap on the car's bonnet. Zarmeena stooped low, placed the car keys on the bonnet, waved quickly at Gul and, without saying or asking any question, went back inside.

Gul swiftly snatched the keys and hopped into the car, wasting no time in heading toward the guesthouse. The drive to the guesthouse lasted a mere twenty-five minutes. Turning into the driveway, she found herself once again captivated by the architectural beauty of the building.

"This is such a stunning place. The owner must be incredibly wealthy," Gul murmured to herself in awe. After parking the car and turning off the engine, she pondered her next move. "What should I do now?" Her mind was racing.

Suddenly, an idea struck her.

Clutching the bag containing the dress, she entered the guesthouse, attempting to exude confidence even though her heart was pounding in her chest. To her surprise, the guesthouse was abuzz with liveliness. The bustling crowd in the lobby hinted at the commencement of the polo tournament festivities. Gul was immensely impressed by the stunning interior of the guesthouse, and her eyes were drawn to a magnificent mural-sized painting behind the main desk, leaving her breathless. For a few moments, she was completely absorbed in admiring the masterpiece, momentarily forgetting her purpose for being there. Her sense of awe was abruptly interrupted by a tap on her shoulder. Startled, she turned around to find herself face-to-face with a woman. Gul stood there in silence, her mouth agape, momentarily at a loss for words. The woman smiled, clearly puzzled by Gul's expression as if she were encountering a stranger. It was only when Farah waved her hand in front of Gul's face that she snapped back to reality.

"Hello there, Palwasha. Are you all right? You look like you've seen a ghost," Farah asked. It was at that moment that Gul realized that this woman was the same one she had seen with Palwasha on the day of the picnic. Quickly gathering her composure, Gul flashed the lady her most charming smile, attempting to mimic her sister's demeanor.

"Oh, hi! I just came to check if we could have the photo shoot on Saturday instead of Sunday and also to confirm if the other girls will be joining us," she said, maintaining an expectant gaze. Gul twirled a loose tendril of hair between her fingers, a habit she had observed in Palwasha. For a moment, it felt as if Farah's penetrating gaze could see right through her act, but Gul maintained her cool and met Farah's gaze with confidence.

After what felt like an eternity, Farah finally responded, "Dear, I already texted you the date and time, and it won't be possible to change the day. As for the other girls, it's their choice whether they come back or not. Now if you'll excuse me, I have a meeting to attend." She looked at her watch.

Gul hesitated, trying to think of something but thought it better to get out of Farah's penetrating gaze as quickly as she could. "Ah, thank you, Farah. I didn't check my phone for any messages, but I will double-check." And with that, she nodded and hurriedly walked out to her car without once looking back. Farah stared at the retreating figure of the girl, sensing something odd about her behavior. However, with other pressing matters to attend to, she went back to the banquet hall.

Sitting in her car, Gul tried to calm her nerves when a sudden knock on the window made her jump. "Gosh, Najeeb!" she exclaimed, her hand instinctively flying to her face in reaction. "You scared me! What are you doing here?" It was unfortunate that she had run into him on the same day she had canceled their lunch plans. She cringed at the thought but maintained a straight face, looking at Najeeb somewhat defiantly.

"Well, I could ask you the same question," Najeeb retorted, his hands in his pockets as he peered down at her with a mixture of surprise and indignation. "Gul, if you were planning to come here, you could have told me. We could have had lunch together." There was a hint of annoyance in his voice.

Gul found herself in a difficult position, feeling embarrassed and regretful about the situation. She didn't like being a flake, yet here she was, caught somewhat red-handed. Gul was never one to shy away from admitting her mistakes. Taking a deep breath, she looked Najeeb straight in the eye and spoke sincerely. "Look, Najeeb, I shouldn't have ignored your call. Something unexpected came up, and I had to come here instead. I'm sorry." There, she said it, acknowledging her error. For a moment, Najeeb observed her intently. She was honest and direct and always spoke her mind and that's what he liked about her, so instead of getting annoyed, he just threw his hands in the air and stepped back, giving way to Gul to turn her car around. Gul hesitated for a moment, not sure whether to stay and explain further or to just shut up and drive and she decided for the latter. Throwing a quick smile at Najeeb, she drove down the driveway and out of the gates.

Najeeb had sensed that Gul was hiding something or something was bothering her, but he was also sure that in due time, Gul would tell him.

But what if she doesn't? The thought didn't sit well with him. *Well, if she doesn't say anything, I'll have to ask her myself!* He made up his mind.

Turning his attention to the first order of business, he went inside for his meeting with Farah. Upon entering the guesthouse, he went straight to the front desk. The receptionist greeted Najeeb with a familiar, welcoming smile, recognizing him as a regular at the guesthouse. Najeeb returned the gesture with a nod and politely requested to see Farah.

"Of course, sir," the receptionist replied courteously. "Please wait in her office, and I will inform her." He pointed toward the door labeled with Farah's name. Leading the way, the receptionist guided Najeeb to a small yet tastefully decorated office, adorned in gold and black accents. Each time Najeeb visited, he couldn't help but be impressed by the office's elegance, just like the first time.

She definitely has good taste, he thought, gazing at the magnificent life-size painting displayed on the wall. The artwork depicted a graceful elderly man dressed in a suit seated in a wheelchair next to a beautiful young girl. Najeeb presumed the man in the painting to be Farah's father or grandfather. The vibrant colors and meticulous brushstrokes showcased the artist's talent, providing a smooth texture to the artwork. Najeeb, still admiring the painting, took a seat in the leather chair across the desk when a knock on the door interrupted his thoughts, revealing a waiter carrying a tray adorned with bite-sized sandwiches, lemon ginger tarts, and a bowl of locally produced strawberries. The waiter poured the tea and placed it on the coffee table for Najeeb then silently withdrew. Najeeb eagerly yearned for a hot cup of tea, hoping it would alleviate the dull ache that had begun at the base of his neck.

As he waited for Farah, he reviewed the message from Ali concerning Baaz and Khalil's recent movements:

> The two men have departed Balakot. En route to Chitral.

Acting on impulse, he swiped his screen to access the Contacts icon and dialed the number from which he had received the anonymous tip the previous night. He had little hope of any response, and just as he was about to press the red button to end the call, the bell on the other end started ringing. In that moment, his heart skipped a beat. He sat up straight with anticipation, waiting for the person to pick up the phone.

"Pick up. Pick up," he urged, his excitement mounting. But then something peculiar happened. He could hear the ringing of a phone, but it wasn't coming from the other end of the line. Perplexed, he swiftly disconnected the call and hit the redial button, his eyes darting towards the door. Once again, he heard the ringing sound, but strangely enough, the sound emanated from the room itself. Najeeb's disbelief and excitement got merged into a whirlwind of confusion. He disconnected the phone again and pressed the Redial button. By now, he had abandoned his tea, leaving it forgotten on the table. Holding the phone like a metal detector, he moved around the room with an almost possessed determination, searching for the source of the ringing. He circled the desk, and the ringing seemed to be radiating from that area. Attempting to open the drawers, he discovered that the top one was locked. He leaned in, pressing his ear against the desk, trying to pinpoint the origin of the sound. Not finding the source in the drawer, Najeeb grew increasingly frantic as time was running out, knowing that Farah could enter at any moment. The ringing persisted, but the phone seemed elusive. Frustration surged through him until his attention was caught by the black and gold pencil holder on the desk, adjacent to the paperweight. It vibrated ever so slightly as if something inside was causing it to shake. Heart racing with a mix of excitement and trepidation as if he had run a marathon, Najeeb swiftly removed the black-colored pencils, and there it was—a black Nokia phone, incessantly ringing with his own number blinking away. His mind raced as he hurriedly disconnected the call and deleted the missed call log from the Nokia. As he was returning the phone to the bottom of the holder, he heard Farah's voice outside. She was engaged in conversation with someone. Hastily, he pushed the pencils back in place and slid across the desk just as Farah entered the office. Najeeb stood there, heart pounding, clutching his now-cold tea, admiring the painting.

Farah walked in, offering an apologetic smile. "Sorry to have kept you waiting, Mr. Najeeb. I hope you liked our refreshments," she said, eyeing the sandwiches and other treats that remained untouched. Najeeb greeted her and returned the smile, placing his teacup back on the coffee table.

"The tea was lovely. Thank you," he said, taking a seat on the leather sofa. "In fact, I was admiring the painting." He nodded toward the artwork. "It's a masterpiece. Is it you and your father?" attempting to engage in light conversation to soothe his frayed nerves. Little did she know what had just transpired in the room. Farah nodded, her gaze filled with affection as she looked at the portrait.

"Yes, that's me and my father, and in fact, the artist is my mother," she replied, radiating with pride. "She was an amazing artist." She took her seat behind the desk, still gazing at the painting with a distant expression on her face. Najeeb observed her closely, realizing that she had drifted off into the past, lost in her memories. He remained silent, attempting to uncover any potential connection between Baaz, Khalil, and Farah. However, he found himself at a loss. Of all the people, he could never imagine the sophisticated Farah having any links to criminals. The situation was utterly baffling, but he had stumbled upon a vital lead and was determined to pursue it.

Taking a deep breath, Farah refocused her attention on Najeeb. She leaned back in her chair, softly drumming her fingers on the desk's surface. "Well, Mr. Najeeb, how can I help you today?" Her unwavering gaze fixated on his face, causing a slight discomfort within Najeeb. Despite the perspiration gathering under his shirt collar, he maintained his composure.

Clearing his throat, he shifted forward in his chair. "Ah, yes. I wanted to follow up on the status of the rooms we requested and see if you could also provide the blueprints of the building to ensure the security of our VIPs," he responded, his words flowing without pause as he took a sip from his cup, desperately trying to relieve his dry throat. The taste was dull, but he quickly finished it off in two large gulps, his gaze fixed on Farah with anticipation.

Farah nodded, a smile forming on her lips. "Certainly," she replied, turning to her laptop and pressing a few buttons. "We will have five suites ready for your guests. All you have to do is email me their names as soon as possible." Her attention was focused on the screen.

"Of course," Najeeb agreed, his attention focused on her.

"And, Mr. Najeeb, you will be required to make the payment once the booking is confirmed—that's our policy. And as for the blueprints, unfortunately, we cannot provide those. If I recall correctly, this matter was not discussed in our previous meeting," she added, her expression now curious as she looked at him.

Najeeb was aware that his request for the building's layout was a sudden and unplanned move, driven by what he had discovered in the office just moments ago. He wanted to gauge Farah's reaction and see how she would respond.

Clever and evasive and calm as a cucumber, he thought. He still couldn't fathom her involvement in any illicit activities.

"Mr. Najeeb, is everything all right?" Farah called out, noticing his puzzled expression. "You seem lost." She watched him intently, awaiting his response.

Najeeb shook his head, giving a small laugh. "Of course I am. It's just so much work before the tournament and so many details to look into. One feels a bit overwhelmed. I'm sorry if I seemed a bit rude. My apologies."

Farah waved it off with a smile and turned back to the screen. "No worries. I've requested a hold on your five suites," she informed him, closing the laptop.

"Thank you so very much." Najeeb expressed his gratitude. An awkward silence enveloped the room for a couple of minutes as Farah put away her laptop.

Then breaking the silence, she asked, "Tell me, Mr. Najeeb, is Palwasha your cousin?" The question caught Najeeb off guard, but he maintained his composure, nodding slowly as he looked at Farah.

"Not really—she is a very close family friend but just like family. But how do you know her?" Najeeb responded, his voice filled with a hint of surprise, though he maintained a straight face.

Well, well, well. The girl has kept it a secret from him and her immediate family too? Farah thought to herself.

"Oh, she came with a friend of hers who knows me as well," Farah explained, still trying to gauge Najeeb's reaction. "In fact, you just missed her. She was here to confirm the dates for the photo shoot."

Najeeb suddenly stood up, interrupting the conversation. "Oh well, thank you for all your help. I will email the names soon," he said, bidding his farewell and making his way out to his car. Once inside the car, Najeeb remained oblivious to the breathtaking view of the valley below. The guest house was perched on a hill, and as the sun began to set, the valley was bathed in a mesmerizing orange hue. Lost in thought, Najeeb pondered the occurrence of unexplained coincidences that had left him feeling perplexed.

One thing was certain: Farah knew Baaz and Khalil.

But why is she being so mysterious about it? Why would she provide information about their whereabouts?

Najeeb sighed, massaging his temples as the whirlwind of events left him with a throbbing headache. "I need to check with Ali for the latest update," he muttered to himself, realizing the urgency of the situation.

The light ping of a notification on his phone alerted him; it felt as if fate itself was providing an answer to his question:

Baaz and Khalil entering Chitral tonight.

Though a simple message, it sent Najeeb's heart racing. It was from the same sender, the number glaring at him. Najeeb quickly redialed it, but as expected, the phone was powered off.

Putting his phone away, he gazed up at the building. "Farah, what are you up to?"

He scratched his head. *Something is definitely going on behind that beautiful façade of yours!* Najeeb felt fidgety and on edge. He had to uncover the truth and do it quickly. Ali needed to be informed of everything that had transpired. He dialed Ali's number, the ringing sound echoing in his ear, but there was no response. He tried again and was still met with silence. Annoyed, he disconnected the call and attempted to reach Ali's office. The secretary at the office informed Najeeb that Ali had been called away in an emergency. Concerned about Ali's parents, Najeeb couldn't help but wonder, *What emergency?*

The secretary quickly responded, "Sir, there was a massive landslide just outside Chitral on the main highway. I will let you know as soon as I get in touch with him, and if there's a message, you can inform me."

"Thanks," Najeeb replied before ending the call. As Najeeb processed this significant news, his mind raced with possibilities. "There's only one road entering Chitral from Balakot," he contemplated. *The message I received was explicit about the two men entering Chitral tonight. Have they managed to evade the landslide, or are they still on the highway?*

He reversed his car and headed toward the main road. There was one thing Najeeb was sure about: He had to talk to Gul and Palwasha tonight. After a twenty-five-minute drive, he arrived at his uncle's house, where he noticed three cars parked in the driveway. "Well, that's interesting," he mumbled softly to himself. Making his way around the house, he climbed the stairs to the veranda, where the sound of the television seeped through the screen door. He rang the doorbell, and Zarmeena quickly appeared, welcoming him inside.

"Good to see you, Najeeb. Come on in," she greeted, leading him to the living room.

In the living room, Gul sat on the coffee table, holding the remote and attentively watching the news. Anoosha occupied a corner, quietly engrossed in her laptop, while Palwasha was in the kitchen, silently reheating dinner.

"Najeeb is here, and he will be joining us for dinner," Zarmeena announced a bit loudly. Gul, who was sitting engrossed watching the news, turned, a bit surprised, and glared at Zarmeena, who simply ignored her stare and proceeded to the kitchen to set another place for Najeeb. Najeeb had always been close to the sisters and their cousin Zarmeena as all three families had strong bonds amongst them. So it never felt odd for him to drop by anytime. Palwasha, who had arranged the food on the table, greeted Najeeb with a smile. She had always liked Najeeb and considered him as the big brother she never had.

"It's good to see you. It has been quite a while." She smiled, placing the large round dish of Pilaf on the table. "Come on, girls, the food is ready."

Najeeb looked at the spread and grinned. "Quite a feast you girls have here, and it smells delicious as always," he complimented, pulling out a chair for himself. By now, all the girls had taken their seats except for Gul, who remained sitting on the coffee table, not actively participating in the conversation. Najeeb glanced in her direction, sensing that she might still be a bit put off by their earlier disagreement. He amiably called out to her, "Hey, Gul, you can watch the news later. The food is getting cold." For a few seconds, nobody spoke except for the monotonous voice of the newscaster filling the room.

Gul had the urge to walk out, but she controlled her frustration. It wasn't Najeeb's fault that she was feeling a bit out of sorts. Taking a long, deep breath and forcing a big smile onto her face, she got up and said, "Definitely, I'm ravenous." Switching off the TV, she joined the rest of the group for dinner.

The meal was a quiet affair with intermittent low conversation and the clinking of cutlery. Everyone was hungry, with the food disappearing in no time.

"That was a really good pilaf"—Najeeb sighed with satisfaction—"and I have overeaten." He leaned back and eyed his plate.

"Obviously, nobody makes pilaf like Gul and Palwasha," Zarmeena chirped in, gathering the dirty plates and assisting her cousins in clearing the table. The three girls had established a chore rotation schedule, and tonight, it was Zarmeena's turn to do the dishes, while Gul was assigned the task of preparing *qahwa*. Palwasha and Anoosha had moved to the living room and were engaged in small talk. Although Gul had deliberately avoided direct conversation with Najeeb tonight, he saw this moment in the kitchen as an opportunity to talk to her alone. He sauntered into the kitchen and leaned against the counter, facing her, but Gul remained focused on the teapot, not uttering a word. Knowing her well, Najeeb could sense that Gul was feeling somewhat embarrassed about their earlier confrontation. Chuckling softly, he handed her the strainer and remarked, "You seemed to be very busy today." He eyed her—fully expecting a curt reply.

Gul shot him a piercing look and pointed to the cabinet behind him. "Would you mind?"

Najeeb wanted to say something to her, but instead, he retrieved the mugs from the cabinet and placed them on the tray, still waiting for Gul to explain herself.

But Gul continued with the task at hand, giving no explanation. Taking a deep breath, he turned off the stove as the water was nearly boiling over.

"Gul, I really don't know why you're upset with me, but whatever the reason, I'm sorry, but this attitude of yours is not at all helpful. Please, we need to talk—and talk tonight. It's very important. You yourself said that you wanted to discuss something with me. So please, let's make peace," he finished, looking at her almost pleadingly, appearing tired and worried.

Gul felt a wave of shame wash over her. She had been unnecessarily rude to him, although it wasn't his fault. It was simply her own frustration and annoyance with Palwasha and her growing friendship with Anoosha that had clouded her judgment. She looked up at him, offering his mug of *qahwa*.

"No, I am sorry." She whispered her apology. "Let me just give these to the girls"—she raised the tray—"and then we can talk outside on the veranda."

An involuntary sigh of relief escaped his lips. "Thanks, Gul. I'll be outside," he replied with a quick smile before making his way out.

"Okay, here goes," Gul muttered to herself as she carried the tray into the living room. "Girls, the *qahwa* is ready."

Zarmeena, who was going through a magazine, looked up and noticed that there were only three mugs on the tray. "What about you and Najeeb?" she asked, looking around for her friend. "And where is he? Did he already leave?"

Given the dynamics between her and Najeeb, Gul wanted to tape Zarmeena's mouth shut at that moment, but she kept her cool and replied matter-of-factly, "Najeeb took his and mine outside." And before anyone could ask any more questions, she quickly slipped out. Palwasha winked at Zarmeena, giving her a knowing smile. As she was about to step outside, Gul could hear Najeeb talking to someone on the phone, and by the tone of his voice, she could only guess that it was something serious. Feeling a bit hesitant, she stood just inside the screen door, not wanting to barge in. Almost instantly, Najeeb looked up and motioned for Gul to come out. Still feeling a bit sheepish, she pushed the door open, holding a bowl of dates and offering some to Najeeb. She knew he always liked something sweet after a meal just like her father, and tonight of all nights, there was no dessert. Najeeb had just gotten off the phone, and by looking at him, Gul could tell that he was a bit flustered.

She sat on the easy chair next to him. "Is everything okay?"

But Najeeb ignored the question. Instead, he took the dates from her and popped one in his mouth. "I needed something sweet," he remarked, looking thoughtful. Gul kept quiet, unsure of how to approach the subject of Palwasha without confiding in her sister first. Yet she wanted to get an opinion, and who better than Najeeb? Besides, Najeeb was bound to ask her about the trip to the guest house. Najeeb took a long sip of *qahwa* and carefully placed the mug back on the tray. His movements were slow and deliberate, and as Gul watched him closely, she felt a tight knot in her stomach. She sat very still, without blinking, holding her warm mug for some outward comfort.

"Gul, how well do you know Farah?" Najeeb asked directly. "And no dillydallying, please," he added, a serious expression on his face.

And here it is, she thought, the conversation she had been dreading.

Gul was about to answer him but felt annoyed at his last remark as he seemed to doubt her. However, she kept her voice neutral and spoke slowly as if addressing a child. "I am not going to dillydally, Najeeb. Let me explain first, and then you can give your opinion."

Najeeb kept quiet but continued to gaze at her intently—urging her to continue.

"It's not me—it's Palwasha who knows Farah, and that's what I've been trying to find out, and that is why I went to the guesthouse," she whispered, taking in a deep breath. She paused for a moment, looking over her shoulder making sure her sister wouldn't overhear their conversation. When Najeeb didn't interrupt, she continued, describing how she had seen Palwasha and Anoosha with a couple of other girls at the guesthouse on the day of the picnic. Gul also mentioned Farah's presence and shared details about the rubies she had discovered. Furthermore, she explained how Palwasha had been spending most of her weekends with Anoosha instead of them. It was clear that Gul herself was annoyed.

"Where they go and whom they meet, I have no idea. It feels like my sister is keeping things from me."

Najeeb continued to listen carefully, not missing any detail. Gul paused for a second, awaiting Najeeb's reaction, but his silence made her go on. "And also, thank God Farah mistook me for Palwasha!" she exclaimed in low tones.

Najeeb interjected, "And that's why you were at the guesthouse."

"Yes, that's why I couldn't come to our lunch. I wanted to just snoop around and get some kind of information, but the rest you know. Oh, and I wanted to show you the rubies too," Gul explained.

CHAPTER 14

The Strawberry House

Driving in the dead of the night was something Khalil had never enjoyed. This time, however, it felt different. For quite some time, he had been contemplating his life; years had passed since he last traveled out of the city, and embarking on this journey back to his hometown had caused countless sleepless nights and relentless anxiety. Although living a completely different life among strangers had its challenges, he had learned to accept it. The decision to make this journey back to his hometown was solidified when Baaz informed him about potential customers who were specifically interested in the stones he had acquired from Afghanistan. He knew these stones were the finest he had ever encountered in his illicit gem trade, and he was well aware of the significant sum the beauties could fetch. He wanted to seize the opportunity to bring Rehmat along with him to Chitral. Baaz served as the middleman for his contact customers, and Khalil was certain that Baaz had his own collection of gems to sell. They had agreed upon a fixed percentage for Baaz's assistance in connecting Khalil with potential foreign buyers. Since morning, the weather had turned chilly, and the once cornflower-blue sky had transformed into a somber shade of gray. The intermittent showers had washed away the dust from the city's roads, leaving them gleaming and reflecting the vibrant blue and green lights of the neon signs. Inside the jeep, silence enveloped them, broken only by the swishing sounds of the wipers, moving back and forth across the windshield like diligent algae-eating creatures carrying out their tasks. Khalil's grip tightened on the steering wheel as he continued his journey toward his long-forgotten hometown. Uncomfortably, he twisted in his seat, attempting to suppress the emotions stirred up by memories from the past. The flood of thoughts was abruptly interrupted by the insistent ringing of Baaz's phone. Khalil stole a quick glance at Baaz, who was bundled up in a thick shawl, slouching against the door. Grumbling, Baaz sat up and fumbled through the layers of his shawl to find his phone. With some difficulty, he managed to retrieve it and gruffly answered the call. Khalil remained silent, his gaze fixed on the road, but his attention was caught by the conversation as Baaz's voice grew increasingly excited. After a couple of minutes, Baaz bid farewell with a sense of accomplishment.

"Okay, good. And well done," was all he said before cutting off the line. By now, the rain had reduced to a drizzle. Khalil switched on the radio, carefully adjusting the dial to improve the reception.

"Change of plans. We're taking a detour to Balakot first for a couple of hours," Baaz informed and settled back into his huddled position, seemingly unbothered by the change. Suddenly, the tires screeched loudly as Khalil slammed on the brakes.

"*What?* What do you think you're doing?" Khalil exclaimed, annoyed at the sudden change of plan.

Baaz, caught off guard, nearly hit the dashboard but managed to steady himself. Fuming with anger, he turned toward Khalil and yelled, "Hey, what do you think you're doing? I could have hurt myself on the head, man!"

Rehmat, who was in the back seat, was rudely awakened by the sudden jerk, scared by the commotion, and looked at Baaz with wide, fearful eyes.

"Shut up," Khalil growled, abruptly silencing Baaz's rant. "Don't you dare speak to me like that, and I don't take orders from you or anyone else." Although Khalil was usually a gentle man who rarely lost his temper, the tension of the day and the anticipation of returning to Chitral had been building up inside him. This outburst became a release for the emotions he had been suppressing. Baaz, taken aback by Khalil's reaction, opened his mouth to respond but found himself at a loss for words, closing it again like a fish out of water. The jeep had come to a halt on the desolate highway that led out of Peshawar. Inside the vehicle, the three passengers were each grappling with their own internal battles. For Khalil, it required a great deal of effort to regain control over his emotions, which had suddenly overwhelmed him at the mention of Balakot.

Taking a deep breath, Khalil turned in his seat to face Baaz, who still appeared shaken. His tone remained neutral as he questioned Baaz again. "Why are we stopping in Balakot?"

Baaz looked at Khalil and Rehmat, adjusting his shawl tightly around his shoulders. Leaning back, he tried to create some distance between himself and Khalil.

"There is heavy troop movement tonight from Chitral to Bannu," Baaz explained, "some kind of military exercise. It won't be safe to travel to Chitral tonight due to numerous military checkpoints along the way. So we need to take a detour to Balakot."

This was the longest conversation Baaz and Khalil had exchanged since leaving Peshawar. Khalil remained silent, and Baaz settled back into his previous position with a slight snicker. Rehmat, who had retreated into the shadows during Khalil's outburst, cautiously moved closer and lightly tapped Khalil's shoulder.

"You okay, boss?" Rehmat whispered, being cautious not to disturb Baaz again. Rehmat had never seen Khalil lose his temper like that, and for a few seconds, Khalil seemed like a complete stranger to him. He felt a bit awkward, but he cared for Khalil like a son and wanted to make things better for him.

Rifling through the boxes in the back, Rehmat whispered, "Boss, I bought some leftover pizza," moving closer to Khalil so as not to disturb Baaz, who was now snoring away.

Khalil managed a quick smile, looking at Rehmat affectionately through the rearview mirror. "No, it's fine, Rehmat. I better not eat, otherwise I might feel sleepy and then he might have a heart attack," Khalil joked, nodding toward the sleeping form of Baaz.

Rehmat chuckled. "No worries, boss. I'll keep giving you *qahwa*." Moving back, he poured the hot beverage carefully from a thermos, making sure not to spill it. "And, boss, if you're tired, I can drive. You can take some rest," Rehmat offered, hoping that Khalil would let him take the wheel. Although he had never driven on a road before, Rehmat had practiced driving in the football ground near their house. The deserted roads and the prospect of heading to the valley for the polo tournament made him excited at the idea of taking the wheel. It seemed like a perfect vacation. Rehmat waited with bated breath, crossing his fingers, hoping Khalil would agree to his request. But Khalil knew better. The circumstances were not ideal for taking such a chance.

"Not a chance." Khalil shook his head. "We don't want to end up at the bottom of a ditch. Maybe next time," he consoled Rehmat, patting him on the shoulder, "but you keep the *qahwa* coming." Disappointed, Rehmat made a face and settled back, trying to make some *qahwa* for himself amid the boxes and packages surrounding him.

These boxes are heavy. Baaz must have brought a lot of dry fruits with him, Rehmat scowled, stretching his long legs, trying to make himself as comfortable as possible.

The rest of the drive to Balakot was uneventful. Although the usual travel time from Peshawar to Balakot by car was two and a half hours, the continuous rain had made the roads slippery. Khalil was extra cautious due to nighttime driving, which was particularly dangerous in this part of the country with its hairpin turns and winding roads. As a result, it took them a little over four hours to reach their destination. The needle on the gauge showed a half-full tank, but Khalil couldn't afford to be complacent. He knew that under normal circumstances, they would easily make it to Balakot. However, the weather made him reconsider. If the inclement weather persisted or worsened, they could find themselves in a difficult situation. In these parts of the country, a rainstorm often meant power outages, leaving gas stations unable to operate. Khalil knew he couldn't take the chance of running out of fuel. Muttering to himself, Khalil made a right turn onto the Mansehra Bypass road, guided by the bright yellow and red neon signs of the Shell gas station. Spotting an empty space in front of the pumping station, he parked the car and turned off the ignition. Glancing at Baaz, who remained huddled up in the same position, Khalil couldn't determine if he was asleep or intentionally distancing himself from the others in the jeep. Resigning to the latter assumption, Khalil decided to take his chances.

"We've stopped for gas. If you need anything from the tuck shop, now's your chance," Khalil inquired, not expecting much of a response. Annoyingly, Baaz replied in a polite, almost patronizing tone.

"Just a pack of cigarettes would be fine, thank you."

Baaz didn't even bother to open his eyes. Khalil exited the jeep without uttering a word. Rehmat, sensing that he would be left alone with Baaz, quickly scrambled out of the jeep and followed Khalil.

"Boss, why is Baaz traveling with us? We could have gone to the polo match ourselves. Why go with him?" Rehmat asked, puzzled and curious. He didn't appreciate the way Baaz spoke to his boss. Instead, Khalil gave Rehmat an admonishing look.

"I know we can go to the polo match ourselves, and that's exactly what we will do, so don't worry," Khalil reassured him, signaling an end to the conversation. Khalil had no intention of explaining Baaz's presence to Rehmat. Despite his curiosity, Rehmat decided not to push further, sensing it wouldn't be well received. Back in the jeep, Khalil tossed the pack of cigarettes toward Baaz, who caught it with a grunt. Baaz examined the packaging closely, scowling.

"The local ones, they're bloody cheap," he muttered, "but what the heck." With that, he swiftly removed the cellophane wrapping and placed a cigarette in his mouth. "This is just what I needed." Baaz grinned, taking a long drag from his cigarette and exhaling smoke rings in Khalil's direction.

Back on the road, Baaz turned on the radio, attempting to tune in to the local news channel. "There," he said, carefully adjusting the dial until the transmission became clear and loud, free from background disturbances. The radio broadcaster had just finished the news headlines, and the weather report began. "The summer monsoon rains are quite intense in these areas," Khalil commented, trying to strike up a conversation with Baaz. Instead, he received a wisp of smoke floating in front of his face. Blinking rapidly, Khalil rolled down his window to let the smoke escape. The news segment had ended, and now there was local music playing on the radio.

"We will be staying at the guesthouse right next to the post office," Baaz interjected. Khalil remembered the guesthouse vividly. It was owned by an old German lady who had married a local artisan and had settled in Balakot for good. Fondly known as the "strawberry lady" by the locals, she had introduced the concept of strawberry farming to the area, involving children and women in the activity. Khalil smiled as he reminisced about her. The lady used to live in a large house with her husband, but after his untimely passing, she was left alone. With no source of income, she transformed her residence into a guesthouse. Over time, it had gained popularity among both locals and travelers for its delicious food and the lady's captivating storytelling, whether they were true or fabricated. People visiting the guesthouse thoroughly enjoyed the warm hospitality extended by the strawberry lady. The overwhelming support and love from the locals had led to the growth of both the guest house and the strawberry farming. Unfortunately, fate had it otherwise. As the jeep entered Balakot, the aftermath of the devastating earthquake became evident. The town bore the scars of the tragedy even at this moment. Driving along the familiar roads, Khalil felt a surge of panic engulf him. For a brief moment, he felt the urge of abandoning everything and escaping, disregarding the business, Baaz, and all other responsibilities. The tumultuous thoughts raced through his mind and heart, causing his palms to grow sweaty. Yet deep down, he questioned the pointlessness of such actions.

And then what? he asked himself. *How far and for how long can I run?*

Throughout the journey, Khalil's mind had been in turmoil, battling anxiety and seeking answers to his own questions. Unaware of their arrival, he finally realized they had reached the guesthouse. Down in the valley, the twinkling lights of homes were dimming in the fading darkness of the night. The rays of the sun struggled to shine through the dark clouds that had rapidly gathered from the far north of the horizon. Khalil studied the sky and could sense the impending thunderstorm. At the back, Rehmat was peacefully asleep—dreaming of horses with a gentle smile on his lips. Khalil looked at him affectionately, grateful for the blessing the boy brought into his life. At that moment, he realized that Rehmat was the only family he had left. Khalil didn't disturb his slumber and turned his attention back to the road. Meanwhile, Baaz had already exited the car and was making his way up the road towards the guesthouse. The gates were closed, appearing as if they hadn't witnessed the passage of a car in a long time. They hung on their hinges, burdened by the weight of years. Baaz struggled to open the gates, huffing and puffing until he finally succeeded. Gesturing for Khalil to pass through, Khalil shifted the jeep into first gear and navigated the steep driveway, eventually coming to a stop beneath a grand porch. Taking a moment, Khalil sat in the car, attempting to shake off the flood of brooding thoughts. With a determined shake of his head, he exited the vehicle, feeling tired and drained. He stretched his body to its full height and looked up at the remarkable architecture, still standing tall with its faded grandeur like a solitary witness which had witnessed a devastating loss. Baaz had already crossed the ground and was busy splashing water on his face from a water fountain near a small pergola in the front yard. Khalil walked to the center of the once expansive lawn, where the grass had grown tall enough to conceal a baby. It struck him that these very lawns were once filled with the joyful echoes of laughter, but now they resounded with a haunting silence that sent shivers down his spine. The building itself was in ruins; the entrance that was once a marvel now lay in a pitiful state of collapsed beams. As he surveyed the grounds, he noticed the rose bushes that once adorned the boundary walls had grown wild and unruly. Even the strawberry plants, once tended by the old lady, had vanished. Looking at the dilapidated building, Khalil couldn't help but feel a sense of desolation. It had withstood the devastating earthquake, but the ravages of time had taken their toll, reducing it to a forgotten and battered skeleton devoid of any life or soul—much like Khalil himself. A chilling sensation pulsed through him.

Trying to overcome his curiosity, Khalil called out to Baaz. "It looks like nobody is living here now!" It was more of a statement than a question as he had no idea where the old lady had moved to or if she was even alive. However, Baaz's confident stride through the gate piqued his curiosity. Baaz finished washing his face and approached the porch, pausing to look at Khalil.

"The lady was too old to look after the house, and coincidentally, I happened to be in town. When I heard that she was taken to a hospital, I offered to buy the house. Unfortunately, she passed away, so in a way, I am looking after the house in her memory," he explained, giving a sly smile before entering.

Khalil stood there, mouth open in disbelief at Baaz's callousness. Springing into action, he followed Baaz up the steps as the man opened the lock to the main door. Anger surged through Khalil as he pushed Baaz's shoulder.

"What do you mean by that? How could you steal property from an old woman like that?!" For a moment, Rehmat feared that Baaz would retaliate and strike Khalil, given the intensity of his angry gaze and flushed face.

However, Baaz simply stared at Khalil, his tone menacing as he warned, "Don't ever do that again!"

Rehmat, who had woken up by now, stood next to Khalil, trembling with fear, his heart pounding and eyes filled with terror. Baaz then turned and opened the door, leaving the two men outside. Rehmat tugged at Khalil's shirt, expressing his fear and suggesting they return to Peshawar.

"Boss! Boss, please let's go back. I don't like this man," the boy pleaded, clearly frightened. Khalil immediately regretted losing his temper.

"I am sorry, Rehmat, that you had to see that. It was my fault, and I shouldn't have lost my temper like that," Khalil apologized, gently ruffling Rehmat's hair. "Come, let's go inside. You don't have to talk to Baaz—just stay close to me," he reassured, wrapping his arm around the boy. Rehmat, still feeling uneasy, nodded and followed Khalil into the building. The musty smell and dampness welcomed them as they entered. Baaz had already switched on the lights in the spacious entryway, pushing back the encroaching darkness. Khalil and Rehmat stood in the center of the hallway with wooden stairs leading up to the second floor. Khalil surveyed his surroundings, trying to recall the original beauty of the building, now marred by the passage of time and the forces of nature.

Baaz has taken the building under his possession and that too from a widow on her deathbed, Khalil thought, shaking his head still in disbelief.

"Boss, boss, over here!" The insistent murmur of Rehmat snapped him back from his reverie.

"What?" Khalil inquired, their low tones echoing in the hallway like ghost whisperers.

"Boss, that room," Rehmat tugged at Khalil's hand, pointing to the door on the right side of the hallway.

Khalil followed Rehmat's gaze and noticed the door. It appeared slightly ajar as if inviting them in. Curiosity piqued, Khalil approached the door cautiously. The room beyond was dimly lit with a faint glow coming from the cracked window. As he stepped inside, Khalil's eyes scanned the surroundings. The room was sparsely furnished with a worn-out armchair in one corner and a dusty desk against the wall. Sunlight filtered through the gaps in the curtains, casting elongated shadows on the faded wallpaper. Rehmat stood beside Khalil, peering into the room with a mix of excitement and apprehension. Khalil gently squeezed the boy's shoulder, silently acknowledging his presence. Together, they ventured further into the room, their footsteps muffled by the worn-out carpet. The air in the room felt heavy as if it held secrets and stories long forgotten.

"You guys can rest here. I have to put these boxes in the jeep."

Suddenly, Baaz appeared from a dark corner of the room carrying a load of cartons. With that, he walked back to the hallway. Khalil observed the weight and size of the boxes, realizing that they must have been the reason for the detour to Balakot rather than any army convoys. However, Khalil decided not to question Baaz about misleading him. He would focus on his own business and leave the rest aside. Khalil grunted and walked further inside the dimly lit room. A worn-out mattress lay in one corner, and two chairs with broken armrests were placed in the center. As Khalil surveyed the room, he noticed there were still some boxes remaining. He hesitated for a moment but then resolved to investigate further. Slowly, he made his way toward the boxes, wanting to see what was inside them. But to his disappointment, they were securely taped, preventing him from satisfying his curiosity. He moved back, knowing he wouldn't be able to open them. Just as he was about to give up, he heard Baaz returning.

"Well, it seems you don't fancy the accommodations here," Baaz laughed, looking around. "Help me with the boxes, boy." He gestured for Rehmat to assist. Encouraging Rehmat, Khalil nodded, urging him to go along. Rehmat picked up the boxes and followed Baaz.

With nothing else to do, Khalil made himself as comfortable as possible, leaning against the edge of the mattress and waiting. The entire house had fallen into silence and darkness, and before he knew it, he had dozed off. Rehmat had returned to the room, feeling uneasy as the darkness engulfed him. Glancing at the closed window, he sensed the air becoming more humid and musty. Careful not to disturb Khalil, Rehmat tiptoed to the window and unlocked the latch. He looked over his shoulder, ensuring he made no noise, when suddenly a flash of lightning illuminated the room, followed by a deafening clap of thunder. Startled, Rehmat jumped back, causing the window shutter to bang against the frame. Khalil groaned, turning onto his side.

Without opening his eyes, he grumbled, "You better close the window, or else the rainwater will pour in."

Holding his breath, afraid that his boss would get angry, Rehmat whispered, "Sorry boss, it really scared me—the loud thunderclap." He hurriedly closed the window and put on the latch. "And, boss, it's raining hard now." He was glad to have someone to talk to. "It's looking pretty bad." By now, the rain had started lashing hard as if Mother Nature were venting out its anger without any sign of abating.

"Hmm," Khalil grunted, stretching himself. "Are you hungry?" he asked the boy, patting him on the back. "Let's go and get something to eat!"

The thought of food had pushed the fear of Baaz away, and now, with a thankful sigh, Rehmat followed Khalil out of the room, ready for some action.

Once again, there was a loud clap of thunder, causing the light bulb to flicker briefly due to the power fluctuation. "Here we go again," Khalil remarked, his tone derisive. He knew that such weather conditions usually brought about power outages that could last for hours. The continuous rainfall had also caused a sudden drop in temperature, making it feel a bit chilly. Khalil and the boy walked out onto the veranda, and the sudden chill made Rehmat shudder. The wind and lashing rain were causing the tall trees to flail like banshees, and they could feel the occasional splatter of rain on their faces. Khalil looked around and spotted Baaz sitting in one corner, resting against a pillar and smoking.

"Hungry?" Baaz asked absentmindedly, his gaze fixed on the ominous dark clouds pouring rain with no sign of abating. The lightning rolled across the sky, seemingly cracking the world in half.

"Yes," Khalil answered, tearing his eyes away from the sky.

"The food is in the kitchen on the counter," Baaz remarked, still sitting in the same position, puffing on his cigarette. Khalil glanced at Rehmat, nodding to indicate that he should fetch the food, and settled himself down on the opposite end of the veranda, facing Baaz.

"What's the plan? Any more updates from your source?" Khalil asked, studying Baaz intently.

"Yeah, we'll be leaving tonight as soon as the rain slows down a bit," Baaz replied, looking up at the sky.

"I think it'll be better if we leave as soon as possible because it's going to get worse," Khalil answered, and the two men fell silent. After a few minutes, Rehmat walked out carrying a greasy brown paper bag—a big grin on his face.

"You must be really hungry, the way you're smiling," Khalil remarked, happy to see the boy feeling a bit better now.

"Yes, boss! This smells delicious," Rehmat announced, his mouth watering. He quickly settled himself on the floor next to Khalil and took out the naan and the *chapli* kebab, offering one roll to Khalil and taking a large bite from his own juicy portion.

"How about you? Aren't you going to have any?" Khalil asked, offering Baaz the extra roll from the bag.

But Baaz shook his head. "No, I'm good. I've already eaten," he replied. Baaz shrugged, and for the next fifteen minutes, nobody said anything.

After devouring the thick juicy roll, Rehmat pulled out a dirty roll of paper and was engrossed in what he enjoyed the most. With utmost concentration, he carefully sketched Baaz. The boy's hand moved gracefully across the paper, the pencil strokes bringing to life the intensity of Baaz's eyes. Rehmat turned and looked up at Khalil, lowering his voice as he showed what he was finishing.

"It's Baaz," he said with a mischievous smile. "Although I don't like him, he has an interesting face, that's why." He felt the need to explain it to Khalil so he wouldn't feel bad that he wasn't the one being sketched.

Khalil chuckled softly, winking at the boy. "It's great. Just don't show it to him—he might not appreciate seeing his own face," Khalil joked before shifting his attention back to Baaz.

"Well, what's the plan? The weather is not going to get any better," Khalil pointed out, gesturing toward the heavy downpour that had obscured the landscape.

Baaz grunted and flicked his cigarette, which sizzled and went out on the wet floor. "Do you guys have all your belongings?" he asked, holding the lock and key in his hand.

Khalil looked at Rehmat, seeking confirmation, and the boy nodded eagerly.

"Yes, boss, we didn't leave anything in the room. We have everything," Rehmat replied, his excitement evident. He carefully folded the sketch he had made and tucked it into his shirt pocket. It was late afternoon, but due to the continuous downpour, it felt as if the sun had already set.

The white jeep made its way toward Chitral with Khalil having to switch on the headlights. He drove with extra caution as the rain had made the roads slippery. Khalil maintained a safe distance from the car in front, acutely aware of the hazardous conditions. As the storm intensified, the speed of the jeep gradually decreased. Inside the vehicle, all three passengers remained silent, each lost in their own thoughts, silently hoping for the weather to improve.

CHAPTER 15

Secret Revealed

"Hey, you guys!" Palwasha called out to Gul and Najeeb. "There are some updates about the landslide. You don't want to miss them!"

Gul, who had already shown the rubies to Najeeb, looked at him questioningly. However, Najeeb remained silent. At this point, he didn't want to discuss anything about what had happened at the guest house in Farah's office. He thoughtfully glanced at Gul, not wanting to put them in any danger.

"Look, Gul, you need to trust me on this. It's a good thing you told me everything. I'm proud of you."

"Hey, you guys, are you listening?" Palwasha called out again, her voice tinged with concern. "This doesn't look good!"

Najeeb patted Gul's hand reassuringly. "Don't worry, we'll sort this out." He got up from his seat.

"Fine," Gul responded in a monotonous tone. Najeeb noticed her demeanor, but right now, he had so many other things to look into. It was best to keep quiet about it and not involve the girls if he could help it.

"Let's go," Najeeb urged in a soft voice. "Palwasha is calling us. It looks serious."

Gul nodded slowly, contemplating whether she had made the right decision or not. But it was too late now, and she trusted Najeeb wholeheartedly. It was just his nonchalant attitude that bothered her. Gul got up and collected the empty mugs, not noticing Najeeb's worried expressions. He knew he had to seek help and contact Ali as soon as possible.

Inside, the girls had gathered around the television, where a live news report was showcasing the devastating aftermath of the landslide. The images being shown on the screen were horrifying.

"Can you please turn up the volume?" Gul requested, still holding the empty mugs in her hand. She watched the news intently as the newscaster read out the headlines about the impact of the landslide.

"The torrential rain since yesterday morning and flash flooding has caused a massive landslide on the main Chitral KPK highway, resulting in extensive damage to surrounding properties." The newscaster's voice filled the room, adding to the somber atmosphere. "There is a severe traffic jam, and law enforcement agencies and paramedics are currently at the scene."

The channel began replaying the scenes while displaying emergency service numbers for further information. There was silence in the room as everyone processed the news in their own way. Palwasha got up and turned off the television, visibly upset. She looked at Gul, fear evident in her wide eyes.

"I just realized that Ma and Baba and Aunt and Uncle were supposed to travel today," her voice trailed off as she fought back tears. A sigh of relief escaped her lips. "Thank God they postponed their return home!" Her voice cracked.

The mixture of relief for their parents' safety and the grim reality of the tragedy that had affected countless people overwhelmed them. Najeeb looked around at the gloomy and worried faces, feeling the need to take action.

With a light tone, he called out, "Let's call Uncle Pasha. Gul, could you and Zarmeena please get another round of *qahwa* for all of us?" The room was filled with a sense of numbness as they sat there, but they were relieved to have Najeeb take charge.

Sensing the need to uplift the mood, Najeeb clapped his hands and called out, "Hey girls, come on. I'm calling Uncle Pasha. Let's not show our worry in front of them."

His statement had the desired effect. Palwasha, who had been sitting glumly in a corner, looked at Najeeb and noticed a mischievous smile playing at the corner of his mouth. Realizing that he was teasing them, she picked up a nearby cushion and aimed it at Najeeb. With expert reflexes, he dodged the cushion, but it ended up hitting Zarmeena on the head with a soft plop.

"Oops, sorry, Zarmeena. It wasn't meant for you," Palwasha apologized with a grin on her face. "I was just making him understand that we are a hardy bunch." Palwasha blinked at Zarmeena.

"No problem, dear. I will do the job for you," Zarmeena laughed and raised her hand, still holding the pillow.

However, their conversation was interrupted as Gul shushed everyone. She was now on a call with her father. After exchanging pleasantries, Pasha informed them that they were planning to extend their stay for another week. He also requested Najeeb to move in at their house as he believed the girls would be better off with him being there. With a relaxed demeanor, Najeeb looked at the girls, who were now quite relieved that their parents were safe.

"Well, feeling better now?" he asked, his voice filled with reassurance. The girls nodded, feeling relieved after talking to their parents and knowing that they were safe and okay in Balakot.

"It's a good thing you'll be staying here until they come back. We could use an extra pair of hands to finish our work too," Zarmeena commented, winking at her cousins.

Najeeb laughed, raising his hands in the air. "Oh no, no way! I have other important matters to attend to as you have already seen in the news," he replied, getting a bit serious. He looked around. "Where is Anoosha? She was here when we were watching the news."

"Oh, she's gone to bed. She has some important work to finish, and she has to travel to Islamabad early in the morning," Palwasha announced. She was about to get up, feeling tired and sleepy after such a long day. "I think we should all turn in." She tried to suppress another yawn and rubbed her eyes.

For Najeeb, this was the chance he had been looking for. With Anoosha absent, he only trusted the twins and Zarmeena at this point. Turning his attention toward Palwasha, he gestured to her to sit down.

"Palwasha, please can you give me a few minutes? I need to talk to you…and you two as well," he requested, his gaze fixed on the three faces before him. Gul suddenly felt uneasy, knowing what was coming. She looked at Najeeb with a worried expression. However, he ignored her glance and focused on Palwasha.

"Sure." Palwasha nodded, a bit taken aback by the seriousness in Najeeb's voice. Sitting back on the couch, she looked up at Gul and Zarmeena, noticing Gul's avoidance of her gaze. Palwasha felt confused, sensing that whatever Najeeb was about to say, Gul already knew. Sitting up straight, she turned her full attention to Najeeb. "Go on, I'm listening," she said, her tone now defensive.

Leaning forward, Najeeb cleared his throat and looked around. "What I'm about to ask—" He paused, trying to think of a better way to put across what he was thinking, knowing that Palwasha might react defensively. "No, what I'm about to *request* of all of you is to not get defensive or argue. Rest assured there is a valid reason behind it."

Zarmeena and Palwasha looked both curious and slightly concerned. They had never seen Najeeb look so tense and worried. "Najeeb, what is it? Just tell us," Palwasha urged, squirming in her chair, not knowing what the suspense was all about.

Najeeb nodded and went straight to the point. "Palwasha, please don't go to the guesthouse anymore. It's not safe for any of you," he emphasized, looking at all three girls. A hint of desperation crept into Najeeb's voice. "And please don't ask me the reason as I can't divulge that. You will just have to trust me on this and stay away from Farah too."

The room fell into a stunned silence. Gul braced herself for her sister's reaction, while Zarmeena was left dumbstruck, trying to unravel the mystery behind Najeeb's words.

"What do you mean by that, Najeeb? And who are you to tell me what to do and what not to do?" Palwasha glared at Najeeb. Angrily she turned to her sister, who was still standing in the corner, and seeing the look on Palwasha's face, she immediately regretted not confiding in her sister earlier. But now the truth was out, and she would have to face her sister's wrath head-on. Gul met Palwasha's gaze, trying not to flinch as Palwasha stormed over to her, her face red with anger.

"I knew something was not right!" Palwasha was shaking with emotion, her accusatory gaze shifting between Najeeb and Gul. "You, Gul, you put him up to it." She pointed her finger at Najeeb, her voice filled with anger. "You could have come to me and asked me directly."

Najeeb stepped forward, blocking Palwasha's path as she tried to leave the room. His tone was firm and serious. "Enough, Palwasha! Stop being hysterical and stop blaming your sister. I am here because your father put me in charge of all three of you, and you better listen to me when I say don't go to the guesthouse. It's not safe, and it's under investigation!" Najeeb added the last part, knowing it wasn't entirely true, but he wanted to emphasize the seriousness of the situation. He knew it wasn't long until Farah would be called in for questioning.

Taking a deep breath, Najeeb shook his head, trying to regain his composure. He looked at Palwasha, pleading with his eyes. "I am sorry for the way I spoke but please, trust me on this. Your sister would never say or do anything that could put you in harm's way. Give me time, and I will personally take you to the guesthouse when I feel it is safe, but"—he paused, looking at everyone—"right now, it is out of bounds for all of you. And now, if you all could excuse me, I have some important and urgent work to attend to." He pointed to the headlines on the television, which once again displayed the destruction caused by the landslide. "I am going to the office, and yes, I will be staying here." He reminded them that he was in charge until their parents returned from Balakot. Shooting a glance at Gul, who was standing with her head slightly bent forward, staring at something on the floor, Najeeb decided not to say anything to her at the moment. He made a mental note to talk to Gul once he returned from the office. With a final nod to the three girls, Najeeb turned and left the room, his mind already occupied with the tasks ahead. Zarmeena, who had preferred to stay out of the situation between her two cousins, sprang into action. She quickly moved to the study table, pulled open the drawer, and retrieved a spare set of keys to the house.

Handing them to Najeeb, she called out, "Here, take this. It's the spare key to the front and back door. You should have it." With that, she placed the keys in his hand and returned to her seat.

"Right," Najeeb commented, looking at the keys as if seeing them for the first time. "Thanks, and I'll be in my office, just a phone call away. So good night." With that, he left the house and jogged back to his car. Najeeb noticed that his phone was on silent and there were several missed calls from Ali.

That certainly doesn't bode well, he thought, feeling a sense of unease. Something must be terribly wrong; otherwise, Ali, the friend he knew, was certainly capable of handling any kind of situation efficiently. "I have had enough for tonight!" he muttered while reversing the car out of the driveway and onto the main road. He tried calling Ali, but the number was busy. Najeeb hoped there were no fatalities due to the landslide, but he knew deep down that this was too good to be true. Such accidents often resulted in a number of casualties along with the destruction of land and property. Najeeb couldn't comprehend how so many things were happening all at once, especially when the biggest polo tournament in the valley was just around the corner. *We have to move—and move fast,* he thought, gripping the steering wheel tightly. The valley and its people could not afford a setback of such magnitude, which could hinder the progress they had made in the previous couple of years. Frustrated, he tried calling Ali again, but there was still no response. Thinking quickly, he dialed his office, gathering all the available updates regarding the accident. Najeeb instructed his office to deploy additional law enforcement personnel and machinery from the neighboring town to assist with the search-and-rescue process. With that taken care of, he switched on the radio to the local news channel, eager to get the latest updates on the situation.

Back in the living room, the atmosphere was strained. Palwasha, still reeling from the unexpected revelation, stood motionless, lost in her own thoughts. Gul observed her sister's expression, feeling remorseful for not discussing the matter with her beforehand.

Approaching Palwasha cautiously, Gul attempted to apologize, but before she could finish her sentence, Palwasha interrupted her, her eyes welling up with tears and a tone of bitterness in her voice.

"Thank you for nothing," she spat out, hurt evident in her tone. "If we fail to meet the deadline, it will be entirely your fault, and the exhibition won't happen." With that outburst, Palwasha stormed out of the room. The abrupt departure left Gul and Zarmeena feeling disheartened and unsure of how to mend the situation. Gul's intention had never been to hurt her sister or jeopardize the exhibition, but it seemed that was exactly what had happened. She longed for reassurance from her cousin, but Zarmeena herself was at a loss for words.

"What were you thinking, Gul? Going behind Palwasha's back like that? You need to talk to her and clear up the misunderstanding between the two of you!" Zarmeena let out a loud sigh, shaking her head. "We can't afford to have such fights right before the exhibition. The tension between the two of you will undoubtedly affect our work."

Her eyes brimming with tears of regret, Gul squeezed her eyes shut, thinking of the exhibition and the responsibility they had toward their workers. "Gosh, I did not mean for all of this to happen. I should have talked to Palwasha first."

Palwasha, who had left the living room in a huff, was seething with anger in her room. The realization of the consequences of her argument with Gul started to sink in. She was overwhelmed by the thought of having to face Anoosha and explain the situation, knowing that Anoosha had put in a lot of effort to secure the modeling assignment for her. And Najeeb's order to stay away from the guest house only added to her frustration. Palwasha paced back and forth in the room. Feeling betrayed, she thought, *Gul felt more comfortable talking to Najeeb instead of confronting me directly?* The question made her uncomfortable, and she felt hurt that her own sister had gone behind her back instead of taking her in confidence. Mentally exhausted, she thumped into bed as a sense of unease swept over her.

Something is off. The secrecy surrounding the guesthouse compelled her to replay the day of the photo shoot in her mind. *Where were the models that day? And why aren't they responding to my calls and texts?* The absence of her friends from the group, especially Hina's unresponsiveness, added to her confusion. With wide eyes, she lay in the darkness; the mysteries surrounding the guesthouse and the alleged investigation Najeeb mentioned nagged at her. But despite all these uncertainties, Palwasha knew she had to stay focused on the exhibition.

Without the money from the modeling project, we'll be back to square one. She felt alone.

Palwasha's thoughts were disrupted by the light creak of the bedroom door. The light from the hallway revealed a meek Gul, who tiptoed in, hoping to talk to Palwasha. Even in the dim glow of the night light, she could make out the haphazardly thrown cushions on the floor and the crumpled duvet cover on one side of the bed. Carefully, she picked up the cushions and placed them aside. Approaching the bed cautiously, she peeked down at Palwasha, sensing her sister's upset, though it was unclear whether she was awake or asleep.

Should I wake her up or is she pretending?

Unsure, she decided to take the chance and gently placed her hand on the covered form of her sister. "Palwasha, if you're awake, please just listen to me. I need to talk to you," she whispered. But there was no response. Gul looked at her sister's unresponsive form intently and sighed. "All right, if you don't want to talk tonight, I understand. We can talk tomorrow…and just so you know, I'm terribly sorry for what happened downstairs." With that, she moved away from the bed and quietly went to the dressing room to change for the night, feeling somewhat deflated. When Gul returned, she found Zarmeena already prepared for bed, sitting very still on the sofa.

"Gosh, Zarmeena!" Gul exclaimed, her hand covering her mouth in surprise.

"What?" Zarmeena whispered from the shadows.

"You scared me, sitting there like a zombie in the dark," Gul replied, walking up to her cousin and looking down at her. "Move over." Gul pushed Zarmeena to make room for herself.

Both girls sat in silence, gazing at the sleeping form of Palwasha, each contemplating how to make peace with her. After a couple of minutes of silence, Zarmeena grew impatient. She glanced sideways at Gul, "Well, what next?" she asked, brushing her long hair and counting the strokes. "One…two…three…four…"

"Stop that, Zarmeena," Gul hushed, nudging her cousin with her elbow. "You don't have to count like a five-year-old. I'll talk to Palwasha in the morning."

"Hmmm good," Zarmeena acknowledged under her breath, resuming her brushstrokes. "Five…yes, five…six." Suddenly, a loud clap of thunder interrupted her count, and she looked at Gul as if she were responsible for the storm outside. The rain had started, creating a drumming sound on the slated roof.

"It sounds bad," Gul commented, ignoring Zarmeena's look, shuddering at the sudden thought of those who were trapped or injured due to the landslide. "It's definitely going to affect the rescue operation," she remarked, thinking of Najeeb and all the law enforcement personnel working round the clock.

"Feels like a bad omen." Zarmeena shuddered, fluffing the pillow and settling herself comfortably as Gul got up to get under her bedcovers. Gul glanced at Palwasha, who was sleeping soundly.

Tomorrow we will talk, and things will be okay between us, she thought to herself, turning toward the window and watching the rain lash against the windowpane.

CHAPTER 16

Peaceful Slumber

It came suddenly out of nowhere. There was this huge shuddering noise, which felt distinctly familiar, but before he could comprehend what was happening, the jeep swerved out of control. The oncoming cars tried to avoid it but failed. The crash seemed to take forever, and at that time, Khalil couldn't do anything. The jeep skimmed and then rolled over with the headlights doing cartwheels. Khalil tried his best to regain control of the steering wheel, but it felt as if it had a power of its own, possessed by some supernatural force. However, the most painful thing was the seat belt, tugging hard against him, straining against his weight, preventing him from bouncing around in the car like a pinball. The strain of the belt was almost suffocating, taking the breath out of him, and then everything suddenly stopped just as abruptly as it had started…except for the sound of the rain.

Khalil found himself drifting in and out of consciousness. It felt like he was traveling between darkness and light, his awareness flickering. Due to sheer luck, the jeep had rolled a couple of times and eventually came to a rest on a grassy knoll. There was a loud shuddering sound, and then everything went black. When Khalil regained consciousness, the first sensation he felt was excruciating pain. He attempted to move but immediately stopped as a wave of agony shot through his body. It became clear to him that he had fractured his ribs—even breathing caused him to gasp. Slowly and cautiously, he tested his arms and legs, relieved to find no further broken bones. He had no idea how long he had been unconscious, but the light breaking through the ink blue darkness on the horizon indicated that a significant amount of time had passed. It was almost dawn, and Khalil considered it a miracle that he had survived the crash.

"Those idiots were driving on the wrong side of the road," he muttered to himself, unaware of the impending landslide. Slowly, he unbuckled his seat belt, which snapped as if it couldn't bear the strain of restraining his body any longer. The release of the belt caused him to gasp in pain as his ribcage jerked slightly. He remained still for a couple of minutes, trying to catch his breath. Gradually, he began to realize that he was not alone when they had left Peshawar.

Rehmat…where is Rehmat? his mind screamed. He remembered Baaz sitting next to him in the passenger seat, but Rehmat's whereabouts were uncertain. Pushing himself up against the seat, grimacing with effort, Khalil looked back, only to be struck by another wave of pain shooting through his side. And then everything came crashing down.

"No…no…no, *no!*" Khalil's voice echoed with despair. "No, please, not again!" His world seemed to crumble around him once more. Overwhelmed by anguish, he behaved like a madman, letting out a howl of rage. With all his strength, he strained against the door, which finally burst open, causing him to fall to his knees amidst the wreckage and swirling dust. With an anguished scream, he stumbled to the back of the jeep and pried open the back door, collapsing inside. There, Rehmat lay amid the jumbled boxes with fruits and sweets scattered on the floor. He appeared to be sleeping, his face peaceful as if he had succumbed to slumber and was dreaming the dream he had always desired. However, the spreading red stain on the front of his shirt told a different story. A pointed shard of glass had pierced his neck, draining the life from his body. Khalil crumpled into himself, releasing a choking sob. With unsteady fingers, he shook the boy in a last-ditch effort to make him move, to see his lopsided smile once again, but there was no response. Numbness enveloped Khalil; his mind went blank as to what to do next. However, his attention was drawn to a bloodstained paper sticking out of the boy's shirt pocket. His hands trembling, he slowly retrieved the paper, unfolding it to reveal an unfinished sketch of Baaz. With unseeing eyes, he flipped it over and gasped. It depicted a polo match with a man and a boy walking hand in hand on one side. Khalil's mouth went dry as if someone was suffocating him, and tears streamed down his face. He sobbed into the boy's chest, his hands clutching the lifeless body, rocking back and forth. The world faded into a blur as a wave of excruciating pain surged through his body, plunging him into darkness as he slipped into unconsciousness.

CHAPTER 17

Chaos

Najeeb made his way to his office, fully aware that it would be a long night ahead. Chitral, after years of internal turmoil, had now regained its position in the news whenever tourism was mentioned. The annual polo match, which had lost its prominence during the unrest, was now back with full glory. Dignitaries from the country and abroad were scheduled to attend, attracting media and reporters from all over, who seemed to be scattered everywhere in the town. The phone continued to ring incessantly as news of the landslide spread. Najeeb called in his assistants for a meeting, eager to gather information about the ongoing search-and-rescue operations. Despite their fatigue, his team displayed dedication and readiness to make a difference in the challenging circumstances. Najeeb knew that the coming days would be long and demanding.

"Please refrain from speaking to the media," Najeeb instructed his team. "Our priority is to complete the work as soon as possible. I am grateful to all of you for putting in these long hours, but our task is not yet finished. The people affected by this disaster rely on your motivation and determination to restore normality."

Taking a moment to compose himself, Najeeb added, "Make sure to call your loved ones at home. I don't want anyone's mother or wife giving me a piece of their mind for keeping you all away for so long." The team chuckled and dispersed to carry out their assigned tasks.

As Najeeb was putting on his coat, his phone rang again. It was Ali, urging him to come to the general hospital as soon as possible. A rush of adrenaline coursed through Najeeb as he hastily replied, "Okay, all right, I got it. I'm leaving right now and will be there in fifteen minutes tops." He hung up, grabbed his wallet and car keys, and practically jogged from his office to his car. Driving toward Mall road, Najeeb encountered heavy traffic due to the accident and roadblock. As he waited at a red light, he could hear the wailing sirens of ambulances. Within minutes, five ambulances with their sirens blaring raced past in the opposite direction, heading out of the city.

God help us all. He shuddered, his mind consumed with thoughts of the injured and the deceased. *What a disaster.*

He glanced up at the sky, which displayed a serene blue hue, devoid of even a single stray cloud. To him, it felt as if the rain's sole purpose was to wreak havoc, lurking somewhere in hiding, waiting to unleash its wrath on another unsuspecting victim. The impatient honking of a car behind him snapped him out of his thoughts. He realized that the traffic light had already turned green, and his preoccupation had caused a minor traffic jam. Frustrated with himself, he moved forward and drove to the hospital, reaching it in the next twenty minutes. The hospital, originally a large villa perched on a small hill, had a rich history. It had once been a private residence before being donated to the city government, which subsequently converted it into a 150-bed hospital. Najeeb turned right through the gate and parked his car in the ample-sized parking lot. He hastened toward the building, filled with a sense of urgency.

The spacious bedrooms and lounging areas had been transformed into wards for the patients. However, given the current situation, the once expansive hallway, which had an *L* shape, was now overcrowded with patients and their attendants. Some were lying on trolleys, while others were being pushed in wheelchairs. The scene was chaotic, and Najeeb couldn't help but shudder inwardly, silently expressing gratitude that his family members were not among the victims of the unfortunate accident. Navigating his way through the crowded hallway, Najeeb headed towards the reception area. Just as he was about to inquire about using the PA system to call DSP

Ali, he spotted Ali walking toward him, waving his hand to catch Najeeb's attention.

"Najeeb!" Ali called out, motioning for his friend to follow him. Quickly maneuvering through the bustling hallway, avoiding stretchers, wheelchairs, and people, Najeeb caught up with Ali, who was already heading in the opposite direction. Together, they entered another hallway, part of the private wing, and it felt as if they had stepped into a completely different building. The atmosphere was distinct with a subtle perfumed scent lingering in the air. Plush seats lined the hallways, and the paramedical staff displayed a higher level of courtesy and attentiveness.

Najeeb couldn't help but express his surprise. "What a stark difference." Continuing to walk alongside Ali, looking at the numbered doors along the hallway, Najeeb remarked, "Money can buy anything, my friend, and I presume our patient is here in this part of the building?" Najeeb's impatience grew as they kept walking, the sound of muted televisions coming from many of the rooms. "You said you people have found someone who would be helpful in our investigation?"

Ali kept walking.

"*Ali?*" Najeeb called out, abruptly stopping and blocking his friend's path. He was becoming frustrated with the secretive approach Ali was taking. Before Najeeb could say anything further, Ali simply pointed toward the second-to-last door on the right-hand side. Following Ali's gaze, Najeeb's eyes fixated on the door marked "Room 14." He stood there until Ali nudged him forward. Taking the cue, Najeeb moved towards the door, intending to knock. However, the door unexpectedly swung open, revealing a plainclothes man standing inside. The tall man nodded at Ali and allowed the two men to enter the room while he stood guard outside. The room they entered was plain yet comfortable with a two-seater leather sofa pushed against one wall. The eye-catching piece was an abstract painting hanging above the sofa. A small coffee table with a few magazines stood in front of the sofa and a wall-mounted television faced the patient's bed. Najeeb quickly surveyed the room, his gaze eventually settling on the person lying in the bed. At first glance, it appeared that the man was sleeping, but upon closer inspection, it was evident that he was either heavily sedated or unconscious. The steady rhythm of the monitor provided a continuous beep, recording the patient's vital signs. Najeeb looked at Ali, his eyes filled with questions. Without uttering a word, Ali gestured for him to take a closer look. With soft steps, Najeeb approached the bed, gripping the icy cold guardrail. He leaned in, studying the unconscious man's face. The swelling and bruises made it challenging to recognize him at first, but there was a nagging sense of familiarity. As Najeeb continued to stare, trying to jog his memory, Ali quietly approached his friend.

"Recognize him?" Ali asked.

Najeeb nodded, his voice a low whisper. "It's Khalil. The injuries make it difficult, but I can see it now. But what about Baaz," Najeeb questioned anxiously, "and how did you find him?" There were so many unanswered questions, but the appearance of Khalil was definitely a stroke of luck. However, they still needed to find Baaz and the missing artifacts. Najeeb contemplated this as he looked at Khalil lying on the bed.

Ali pulled Najeeb to a corner of the room near the window. "It was pure luck that we found him at the accident site. But we need to locate Baaz quickly. With all the chaos, he could easily find a way to hide or leave the area." Ali expressed his concerns to Najeeb. "We require all the resources and manpower that the city government can provide."

Najeeb nodded. "Don't worry, Ali. Our departments are working together until this is resolved. But we need to act swiftly, especially considering that this man is currently unconscious," Najeeb pointed toward Khalil, almost as if Ali was unaware of his condition.

"Seriously, man," Ali interjected, cocking his head to one side, "this information is news to me."

Najeeb gave a lopsided smile, raising his hand in the air, gesturing to Ali. "I was just making sure."

Ali chuckled and sat down on the sofa, looking up at Najeeb, "The bad news is, buddy, you look like hell. But the good news is you look better than our friend here." Ali was known for his ability to crack jokes even in the most trying of times, which made him popular among his peers and juniors. Despite their contrasting approaches to life, their friendship had blossomed into a deep bond of trust and respect that many could only dream of having in a friend.

Najeeb smirked and playfully retorted, "I know, but how about the more important things other than my looks?"

Ali nodded and continued, "Well, their car was hit by a boulder during the landslide, and the jeep fell into a ditch."

"And what about Baaz?" Najeeb asked, his anticipation growing by the minute, but the look on Ali's face told him a different story, and he clenched his fist, waiting for the worst.

"Lost him," Ali replied dejectedly.

"Lost him! But did you find the artifacts? And where is his body?" Najeeb cried out, his mind spiraling out of control.

"Hold your horses, Najeeb. I said we lost him, meaning he fled the scene, disappeared, vanished, abracadabra—nobody, nothing," Ali ranted, voicing whatever came to his mind. For a few seconds, Najeeb thought Ali had lost his mind or that he was too overworked to think straight. He looked at Ali incredulously when he finally realized what Ali was actually saying.

"He escaped?" Najeeb let out a sigh. *This man has the luck of a cat*, he thought.

"There was a third person too with them," Ali added.

"A third person? But the information we received was that only Khalil and Baaz were traveling to Chitral." Najeeb tried to figure out who the third person could be. "And where is that third person? Can't we question him?" Najeeb's optimism began to rise, but he saw Ali shaking his head, which surprised him.

"Dead. The third person was a boy fourteen or fifteen years old, and he died on the spot. We presume he could be related to Khalil—most probably his son," Ali explained.

"And how do you presume that?" Najeeb inquired.

"As far as we know, Khalil didn't have any family." Najeeb looked at Khalil once again, who was still unconscious. Najeeb's attention was drawn to his friend, who had a serious look in his eyes. Instantly, Najeeb became aware that something significant had occurred.

"Ali, what's the matter? There is something else too!" Ali's mood had suddenly plummeted, which was a rarity for him.

Ali looked at Najeeb with a somber expression. "My men, the ones tailing the jeep, were also hit by the landslide, and they didn't make it," Ali informed, remorse evident on his face. "I still have to inform their families." He sat forward, his elbows resting on his knees. "The boy's body has been sent to the morgue for an autopsy. We can order a DNA test to see if it matches with Khalil." Ali was shaken by the news of his men's loss, and they still needed to find Khalil.

Suddenly, he remembered the anonymous phone call to Najeeb. "Hey, I'm sorry I didn't get time to trace the number," he apologized. As he was pulling out his phone, the man on the bed groaned. Ali and Najeeb sat very still, looking expectantly at the patient. Khalil groaned again, this time louder. Ali got up and went to stand next to the bed, hoping the man would come around and they would be able to extract some information from him. The man's eyes were closed, but he was moaning in pain. Thinking quickly, Ali went out of the room to call the on-call doctor. Najeeb, who was standing at the foot end of the bed, once again had the eerie feeling of seeing Khalil somewhere before.

This is really freaking me out. Why is my mind playing tricks on me? he muttered, agitated.

He turned back, thinking of the two dead police officers and the boy. Things had taken a sinister turn now, and his team had to work fast. He looked toward the door, willing Ali to return as quickly as possible with a doctor or a nurse. To his relief, the door opened, and a young doctor walked in, entering the room. Before going to the patient, the doctor ordered Ali and Najeeb to wait outside, and both of them complied. They knew that at this point they would be of no help, and the most important task was to find Baaz.

"Let's go to the cafeteria. It's better to talk there," Ali suggested, leading the way to a small, quaint cafeteria for doctors and visitors. Once seated, Ali looked at Najeeb expectantly. "Well," he prompted, "you were about to say something to me, so shoot."

Najeeb took a sip of his hot coffee and set it down before responding.

"Oh, wait, let me put a trace on the phone number first," Ali interjected, but Najeeb shook his head.

"There is no need. It'd be a waste of time," Najeeb replied, stopping Ali before he could say anything else.

"No need? But why?" Ali quizzed.

Najeeb saw the look, his expression serious. "The number belongs to Farah, the owner of the guesthouse," Najeeb stated, getting straight to the point. He proceeded to recount everything that had transpired in Farah's office and waited for Ali's reaction, maintaining a steady gaze. Ali took a moment to process the name that Najeeb had mentioned. When the realization finally struck him, he looked at Najeeb with a mixture of disbelief and incredulity.

"So you're telling me that Farah was the one giving you the tip?" Ali exclaimed. "Well, well, well, this certainly adds a whole new twist to the investigation. And Farah! Who would have thought that the formidable Farah would be mixed up with smugglers? And on top of that, she's determined to help you, buddy! I wonder why? Maybe I should talk to Gul and ask her to keep an eye on you!" Ali gave a friendly thump on his friend's shoulder.

"You and your presumptions," Najeeb remarked, playfully punching his friend. "Okay, let's be serious. What should be our first step?" Najeeb was eager to move things forward. Then he snapped his fingers, a spark of excitement in his eyes. "Ali, can't you obtain a search warrant for the guesthouse? I'm sure we'll find all the answers there, and Baaz might be hiding there as well." Suddenly, Najeeb felt a surge of hope that they could make progress in the right direction. However, when he looked at his friend, he seemed unimpressed, sitting in the same position as he had been ten minutes ago. "What? Didn't you hear what I just said? And you're just sitting here as if you have all the time in the world." Najeeb was growing impatient.

Ali still didn't react, but he leaned forward in his chair. "That's the way things ought to proceed, my friend," he said solemnly, "and out of all the people, I would love to get my hands on Baaz. I feel guilty that because of my orders, my two men who were tailing these criminals met with an accident and lost their lives. However, unfortunately, in the court of law, we first need solid proof to obtain a search warrant. I was hoping that Khalil could testify against Baaz, and perhaps his statement could implicate Farah as well. So my dear friend, we have to keep our fingers crossed and hope that Khalil wakes up soon." Ali's words carried a sense of determination and concern. Najeeb fell silent, realizing that Ali's assessment of the situation was accurate. Their only hope now rested on Khalil's testimony or the possibility of finding Baaz, who was likely in hiding.

"Hmmm…I'm sorry for jumping the gun, Ali," Najeeb admitted, realizing his impulsive reaction. "I'm sure you've analyzed the case from every angle. Should we go to the ward and see what the doctor has to say about Khalil's condition?" He got up from his seat and patted Ali on the back, receiving a quick smile in return, although Ali's eyes remained serious and focused. Back in the room, the doctor was just finishing giving instructions to a nurse when Najeeb approached him.

After introducing himself, Najeeb asked the most important question: "Doctor, how long do you think it will take for the patient to regain consciousness?"

"Hmm, his vitals are improving, and we hope he will wake up soon, maybe within a day. But if not, there's a chance he could slip into a coma," the doctor candidly informed them, not sugarcoating the potential outcome. "I apologize for the grim possibilities. If you have any further questions, feel free to visit my office." With a nod and handshake, the doctor exited the room, leaving Najeeb and Ali feeling despondent.

"Now what?" Najeeb voiced the question that was weighing on both his and Ali's minds. "If he falls into a coma and Baaz manages to escape the valley, all our efforts and coordination with the authorities would be in vain!"

Ali motioned for Najeeb to follow him, and they walked out of the room. In the hallway, Ali signaled for the guard to enter and then turned to Najeeb. "Listen, I just received a message that one of my men recovered some statues and possibly smuggled gems near the jeep. However, the black onyx statue was not among the boxes that were found." Ali read aloud the message he had received a few minutes ago. This caught Najeeb's attention.

"Wow, with everything that has happened, the man managed to get away with it!"

The black onyx statue of Buddha had gone missing after the invasion of Afghanistan, and it was considered to be one of the most valuable Buddha statues. Now, after decades, there was intel that it had resurfaced, first in Afghanistan and now in Pakistan, making it one of the most sought-after artifacts in the black market.

"Phew...this is incredible, having the most wanted man and the statue in the underworld somewhere in the valley," Najeeb exclaimed, thinking aloud. He leaned closer to Ali, looking intently at him. "Listen, Ali, although it's not my domain, my department would like to help you in any way possible." He paused for a moment. "You guys search for Baaz, and I will try to find out the role of Farah in all this." Najeeb reached into his pocket and handed Ali a small crumpled paper bag. "Be careful with these—the rubies are inside."

Ali, surprised, looked at his friend. It was evident that he wanted to know where Najeeb had obtained the stones. Najeeb quickly fabricated a story about finding the precious gems outside the gates of the guesthouse, purposely omitting any mention of Gul and Palwasha's involvement to protect them from being implicated in the investigation. Ali sensed that there was more to the story as finding the rubies randomly didn't sit well with him. However, he trusted that Najeeb would eventually share the details. Taking the packet, Ali put it in his pocket and gave Najeeb a questioning look, silently asking if there was anything else to add. When Najeeb remained silent, Ali ran his hand through his hair, appearing concerned. "Najeeb, you know that withholding information during an ongoing investigation is a crime," he warned. Taking a deep breath, Najeeb felt relieved that he had bought some time to investigate the situation at the guesthouse.

"Thanks a ton, buddy. I know I can count on you, and don't worry," Najeeb reassured him, his expression genuine and sincere. The two men contemplated whether to stay at the hospital or return, but their thoughts were interrupted by the nurse on her afternoon rounds. She approached them and pointed to her wristwatch.

"Sir, it's way past visiting hours," she stated firmly. Before Ali could respond, she added, "I know this person is in police custody, and you already have a guard inside. So please, you gentlemen need to leave. Thank you." The nurse, though pleasant-looking, had transformed into a matronly figure, ready to wield her authority.

"But, ma'am—" Ali attempted to say something but was swiftly interrupted.

"No ifs and buts, sir. If you want to wait, you can go to the waiting lounge."

Najeeb cleared his throat, casting a glance at Ali. "Ma'am, you are right," he said, addressing the nurse, "but could you do us a favor? Can you call me on this number as soon as he wakes up? It's imperative that we talk to him as soon as possible." Najeeb took out one of his visiting cards and handed it to the nurse.

For a few seconds, she simply looked at him, and Ali thought she might discard the card. However, to their surprise, she broke into a smile, causing her small eyes to almost disappear. "Oh, I know you! You're the new deputy commissioner of Chitral. I saw your photo in the local newspaper. It's high time our local youth take up key positions in the local government. Don't worry, I will definitely call you as soon as there is any improvement in the patient's condition."

Najeeb felt a sense of embarrassment and simply smiled, unable to respond. Ali stepped forward, placing his arm around his friend. "Ma'am, he certainly is a local hero. Thank you for your cooperation."

Outside in the parking lot, both men bid their goodbyes and returned to their respective offices.

CHAPTER 18

The Attic

At Najeeb's office, he received briefings about the ongoing rescue and restoration operations, which were progressing smoothly. After assigning tasks and further discussions, Najeeb found himself lost in thought in his office. He was trying to figure out how to connect Farah's role with Baaz and Khalil when Ali called with disappointing news. The traced number led to a local man who had moved away from the area six months ago. "Our only hope now is Khalil, and if we catch Baaz, it'd be even better," Ali sighed, ending the call.

Najeeb placed the phone on his desk and stared at it as if hoping for answers to appear. *How do I link Farah to all of this? Should I confront her directly? But if she wanted to, she could have approached me openly. Why all this secrecy?*

Questions started piling up but with no reasonable answers. And no matter how he approached the situation, Gul and Palwasha seemed to be in the center of the mess. Twirling the pen in his fingers, he sat there, lost in his thoughts.

What have the girls gotten themselves into? he murmured. Glancing at his watch, he realized it was almost 5:00 p.m. *Time has flown, and we've made no progress.* He sighed.

As an afterthought, he called the nurse to inquire about Khalil's condition. She informed him that there had been no change. "Don't worry, you will be the first to know," she reassured him. Two calls within five minutes and no encouraging news. Reluctantly, he knew he would have to seek help from his cousins. It seemed to be the only way to uncover more information. And thinking of the girls, he suddenly became aware of his own fatigue and hunger. His clothes were disheveled, and his hair was a mess.

Upon arriving at Gul and Palwasha's house, he noticed that the parking lot was empty. No cars were in the driveway.

Strange. Is everyone going in different directions? he pondered to himself.

Sitting in his car away from the noise and chaos of the office, he took a moment to think things through. As the assistant commissioner of Chitral, he had a significant responsibility toward the people and his country. He had witnessed the struggles of the people in Gilgit and Baltistan, and now, just as peace and tourism were flourishing, this smuggling case had surfaced. If word got out that Baaz had slipped through their hands, the media wouldn't take it lightly. At this point, all eyes were on Chitral, and rightfully so: Pakistan had been recognized by the World Economic Forum as one of the top twenty-five global destinations for UNESCO World Heritage Sites in 2019. The sacrifices and hard work put into promoting tourism and preserving cultural heritage would be in vain if news got out about Baaz's attempt to smuggle the renowned Buddha statue during the peak of the tournament season.

Najeeb took a deep breath and stepped out of the car. First, he needed some rest. Then he would call Ali for any updates on the search for Baaz. After that, he would assess the situation and determine what else could be done—with or without the help of the girls. The house was quiet, and by the time Najeeb had showered and changed, his stomach was growling with hunger. Opening the refrigerator, he decided to fry some eggs along with some cheese and toast. His eyes twinkled at the sight of a hand-cut smiley face sticking up with a toothpick from a platter. Chuckling, he carefully took out the plate with the smiley face bobbing up and down.

"That's nice." Najeeb beamed and removed the cellophane wrapping. "Chicken sandwiches, fried chops, and potato salad," he said aloud. "Wow, they really have outdone themselves." He appreciated the effort and looked for a glass to fill it with freshly made lemonade from the pitcher. Grabbing a fork from the drawer, he took his plate and the lemonade to the lounge, making himself comfortable in front of the television. There was a political talk show being aired on the news channel. He listened to the discussions, but scoffed and changed the channel, annoyed with the never-ending mudslinging atmosphere that had become the norm of these shows. Switching off the television, he sat back to enjoy his food with only the familiar ticking sound of the large wall clock over the mantlepiece. As he savored his meal, he looked around and noticed how much had changed over the years. The house had been renovated and some new additions made, but this particular room had always remained the same. It had been the hub of activity, filled with laughter, tears, discussions, and arguments, with the family always staying united there in that room.

Reminiscing about the old days, a slow smile spread over his face. He could almost hear himself and his friends playing in the room as kids—Gul, Palwasha, Zarmeena himself, and even Farishtay and Zarak. The sisters' youngest uncle, Zargul, was the most fun-loving person, and the kids adored him, always gathering around him for fun and games.

Hmmm, good old days. He sighed, getting up and popping the last piece of meat in his mouth.

He didn't want to dwell on those days anymore, so he busied himself with some pending official emails to take his mind off them. Najeeb was so engrossed in his work that he didn't hear the key turning in the lock.

"Oh, there you are. The house was quiet, and I thought you might be sleeping," Gul said as she tiptoed into the living room, assuming Najeeb might be resting. Najeeb looked up expectantly and saw Gul struggling with the heavy bags she was carrying. He quickly got up to help her.

"Whoa there," he said, assisting Gul with the bags. "I thought you girls were working tirelessly at the workshop, but looking at all this stuff, I wonder if you left anything in the shops?" More of the girls entered, carrying additional bags. Najeeb helped Gul with her bags and then proceeded to help with the rest, placing them in the corridor since there was little space left in the lounge. "By the looks of it, I don't think the factory will be making any profit soon," he remarked jokingly, poking at the bags.

"Oh, you and your jokes, Najeeb," Zarmeena responded, playfully pushing him aside to make room for more bags. "Here, can you put these bags in the corner, please?"

Finally, Palwasha entered with a large carton, which she dropped just inside the door. "That was certainly heavy, and you guys are just sitting here," she commented, brushing off the dust from her clothes. "Oh, hi, Najeeb," she greeted her cousin, acknowledging his presence as he helped organize the bags.

After organizing the boxes, Najeeb glanced around the room, still puzzled by the presence of these additional materials. "Well, this certainly feels like a second workshop for you guys," he remarked, seeking an explanation for the boxes in the house.

Gul nodded and replied, "We're planning to put in extra hours, especially for the dresses we'll be showcasing at the exhibition. These bags have all the materials, tools, and accessories we'll need."

Palwasha, having settled herself on the poof, chimed in with a question. "How about things on your end? Is the search-and-rescue operation still ongoing?" She handed everyone some cookies they had picked up from the bakery on their way home. The next hour was spent discussing the landslide and the measures being taken to assist those affected.

"Thank God the fatalities weren't high," Zarmeena interjected.

"You mentioned there were only five people who died in the accident, right?" Gul turned to Najeeb, seeking confirmation.

"Yes, five fatalities and thirty injured, and out of those, seven are in serious condition," Najeeb replied, his knowledge of the situation evident. Gul then asked about the identities of the deceased, wondering if they were tourists or locals.

Before Najeeb could answer, Zarmeena interjected, "That's got to be the worst landslide since the earthquake." The room fell silent as the memories of that tragic event resurfaced, each person reflecting on the emotional impact it had on their lives. Meanwhile, Najeeb had been pondering how to gather more information about Farah discreetly as well as the possible connection between Farah, Baaz, and Khalil. An idea was taking shape in his mind, one that he knew was bold and dangerous, especially considering Baaz's involvement. However, time was of the essence, and conventional surveillance methods would take too long. They needed to act swiftly before Baaz could escape across the border to China or Afghanistan.

Najeeb looked at his cousins, noticing their long faces, and clapped his hands loudly. "Why such long and somber faces?" he exclaimed. "Don't you girls have work to do?" He gestured toward the bags scattered throughout the room. Taking the cue from Najeeb, Gul pulled herself up, determined to shake off the somber atmosphere. She realized that Najeeb hadn't answered her question about the identities of the deceased, but she trusted that he had a good reason for it.

Forcing a smile, she called out cheerfully, "That's right, girls. We need to finish the three main dresses."

With the help of Najeeb and Zarmeena, they began rearranging the furniture to create a workspace. "Hey, Palwasha, get up! What are you doing?" Gul impatiently waited for her sister to move from the poof, which was obstructing the way. Palwasha, true to her dramatic nature, was sitting cross-legged on top of the poof, resembling a Buddha statue. Her eyes were closed, and she began humming with her palms extended upward, as if meditating. "Palwasha!" Gul called out in exasperation.

"I was praying for all our problems to get resolved and for all the work to be done," Palwasha replied, still in a trancelike state, opening one eye and glancing at her sister. However, when she saw Gul's expression, she quickly snapped out of it. "Well, it didn't work," she said, making a comical face. "All my problems are still in the bag!" She pretended to be surprised.

Zarmeena, who had momentarily left the room, returned and started singing loudly, interrupting the laughter-filled atmosphere:

"I faced it all! I stood tall...and did it my...*aaaachooooo*!" She sneezed abruptly, causing everyone to burst into laughter.

Gul, who was trying to arrange the chaos of the bags and the cartons, giggled, looking at her cousin. "You mean you're trying to sing Sinatra's 'My Way,' but you've caught the crooner virus?" Gul chuckled.

"God bless you!" Najeeb commented, joining in the laughter. Najeeb walked over to where Zarmeena was struggling to balance the mannequin on the stand. "Here, let me help you." He took the mannequin from her hands. "A headless mannequin?" he remarked as if it was an alien. "I wouldn't want something like that lurking in my house." He gave an exaggerated shudder.

Zarmeena smirked. "Don't worry—it won't bite. Just put it on the sofa," she instructed. "And Najeeb, can you please get the mannequin's head? It's in the attic upstairs. I don't want to go there—it's quite musty up there." She fanned the air in front of her face. Zarmeena needed the mannequin's head to get some idea of the fit and shape for the headgear she was designing. With a serious expression on her face, she batted her eyes at Najeeb in a comical fashion. Najeeb tried hard not to laugh and simply nodded before making his way up to the attic.

"It definitely is dusty and dark in here," Najeeb muttered to himself as he searched for the switch to turn on the light. Feeling around near the door on the left side, he finally found it and flipped it on. The light was dull and barely illuminated the room, making it uncomfortable to stay. "Oh, what the heck. I just need to find the lost head and go," he reassured himself. Scanning the room, his gaze fell upon some boxes stored on a shelf. Being a tall man, Najeeb had to bend down due to the low ceiling. He carefully pulled the first box down and peeked inside. To his surprise, he found stacks of clear plastic bags filled with photographs. "Oh! What a pleasant surprise," he commented, smiling to himself, pulling out some of the pictures from the top bag. As he sifted through the photos, he came across old family pictures, his uncles, their families, his parents, and himself. "Wow, what a treasure." He swiftly went through them. Among them were images taken at birthday parties with his friends and cousins dressed in different costumes. While still engrossed, reminiscing the yesteryears, his attention was caught by a particular photo. He examined it closely, squinting. "Ah, this picture is lovely." The dim light made it difficult to see. It was a group photo of his grandparents, parents, and Gul's dad, whom he fondly called Uncle Pasha. His gaze then settled on Pasha's younger brother, Uncle Zargul, and he couldn't help but admire how handsome they both looked. Uncle Zargul had always been the favorite of every child in the family. Lost in his thoughts, Najeeb was suddenly jolted back to reality by Zarmeena's loud voice calling him.

"Gosh, I completely forgot about her head," he muttered, annoyed with himself. "Still looking, Zarmeena!" he shouted back, hastily checking the remaining boxes one by one.

"Oh shucks, what is he doing?" grumbled Zarmeena, waiting at the bottom of the stairs for Najeeb to bring down the missing piece of the mannequin. Growing impatient, she called out again, "*Najeeb?*" ready to go to the attic herself.

"Coming!" Najeeb responded, quickly going through the boxes. Finally, he found what he was looking for at the bottom of the last box. "Found it!" He put away the box and switched off the lights as he exited the door. On an impulse, he had also taken the first batch of pictures he had come across, mostly consisting of family photos. He was looking forward to a quiet evening going through the old memories. Carefully descending the stairs of the attic and then the main staircase, Najeeb entered the room with the pictures and the mannequin's head.

"Oh, come on, Najeeb—it took ages. What were you doing—cleaning the attic?" Zarmeena immediately pounced on him, expressing her frustration at his delay. She eyed the cardboard box suspiciously.

"Just your lost head," Najeeb retorted, handing her the box, "and yes, that attic needs to be cleaned"—he dusted off his clothes—"and mind you girls, I am not going upstairs again." He looked for a place to sit down, in the chaotic mess. He then took out the photos and made his way to the recliner that had been pushed to the far corner near the window. "I found some old family pictures and I thought I'd spend the evening going through them."

Gul looked up from her work. "That's nice. Would you pass them around so that all of us can have a look?"

As Najeeb sifted through the pictures, he came across one that caught his attention. Setting it aside, he wanted to examine it more closely. After a while, he placed the rest of the photos back in the box and focused his attention on the particular picture, feeling drawn to it.

Gul, who was sitting across from Najeeb, had been observing him and noticed that he seemed lost in thought. "He seems preoccupied," she murmured to herself.

Palwasha, who was sitting nearby, overheard and playfully nudged Gul. "Pretty sure he's lost in one of your photos." She winked at her sister.

"Palwasha, you and your cheap thoughts." Gul pinched her sister ever so lightly. "Concentrate on your work." With that, she put her diary down and approached Najeeb. "Is everything okay?"

"Yeah, yeah, everything is fine." After a brief pause, he looked up at Gul thoughtfully. "Gul, was this the picture taken just before Uncle Zargul decided to move to Balakot?" he asked, holding it up.

Gul took the picture from Najeeb and examined it closely. "Yeah...I think so," she replied slowly, trying to recall when the photo was taken. "I remember Ma telling me it was taken when he'd come to visit us for the spring festival with his wife and the kids. He was going back to Balakot the next day, and Ba wasn't happy, but he didn't stop Uncle Zargul either." She paused. "It was the last time we saw them...just a few days before the earthquake hit." Gul breathed a deep sigh before asking, "But why are you asking?"

"Oh, nothing, I was just thinking of making an extra copy of it and giving it to my parents. They'd like it," he added nonchalantly. Gul sensed there was more to it than what he was revealing but decided not to press him for answers at that moment. Gul waited for a couple of seconds, but when Najeeb remained silent, she returned to her work. Najeeb, still lost in thought, was jolted back to reality when his phone rang. It was Ali, updating him on Khalil's current condition.

"What? Why did they sedate him?!" Najeeb exclaimed, sitting up in a flustered state. "Were you able to gather any information from him?" He was growing increasingly agitated at how things seemed to slip from their grasp at every turn. Najeeb got up and walked out onto the veranda. Something was not right. Ali was at the hospital and had promised to inform Najeeb as soon as there were any developments. For now, there was nothing else Najeeb could do except wait. The fresh air outside seemed to calm his nerves—even if only temporarily.

"Hey, is everything okay?" Gul had followed Najeeb outside; she could sense whoever the caller was did not bring good news. "All good?" she asked again, sitting next to Najeeb on the steps and wrapping her shawl around her shoulders to ward off the chill. For a couple of minutes, Najeeb remained quiet. Then he sat back, resting against the stairs, and looked thoughtfully at Gul.

"What?" Gul retorted, feeling flustered under his quiet scrutiny. "Why are you looking at me like that?" She inched a bit further away so they could comfortably face each other. Suddenly, she could feel the tips of her ears burning, and an awkward silence hung between them. Trying to avoid his gaze, she began inspecting her toenails.

Gosh, look at your toenails, Gul. Half your nail polish is peeled off. Feeling self-conscious, she curled her toes in and tried to hide them under the long hem of her dress, hoping that Najeeb hadn't noticed.

"That is a pretty color. But the nude color looks prettier on your feet," Najeeb remarked, his voice carrying a hint of a smile. The comment was so sudden that Gul looked up, confused. Najeeb was looking at her toes with a deadpan expression on his face, and when she glanced down, she saw her toes peeking out from underneath her dress.

"Oh, I didn't have time for a pedicure," she responded, almost coyly, and both of them chuckled as she tried to copy Palwasha. The awkwardness that had filled the air seemed to dissolve. Leaning against the pillar, Gul finally asked him what she had been itching to ask. "Now tell me, why are you so interested in that picture?" Silence ensued. Najeeb, uncertain about the hunch he had, didn't want to share anything until he was a hundred percent sure.

"Look, I have a hunch about something, but right now, it seems quite far-fetched. But, Gul, I promise that whether my hunch is wrong or right, I will tell you in due time. For now, just know that

I want to have that photo enlarged for my parents—I'm sure they'll love it." Sincerity resonated in Najeeb's tone, and Gul understood that if he wasn't being entirely forthcoming, there must be a valid reason. She nodded, pulling the shawl more tightly around her.

"I understand, and I hope that whatever difficulty you're facing, you resolve it soon." She assured him, and Najeeb relaxed, knowing he could count on her.

"And one more thing, Gul—I meant to ask you, isn't Anoosha supposed to be staying with you? I haven't seen her around. She was with you girls this morning, and she's not home yet," Najeeb asked out of sheer curiosity.

Gul shrugged. "Well, I don't mind that she's not here. In fact, I feel relieved," Gul retorted, her tone almost hostile. Surprised by her response, Najeeb raised his eyebrows, giving her a questioning look. It was quite unlike Gul to be talking about someone in such a way. "I mean, it seemed like she had wrapped Palwasha around her finger like some little schoolgirl infatuated by a celebrity, and that is so unlike Palwasha," Gul hurriedly explained.

"Gul! I never thought you had a jealous bone in your body! But I'm glad I was wrong and I too have a chance," Najeeb replied teasingly. With that, he got up and walked inside for dinner with a smirk on his face.

As the group cleared up the dinner table, Najeeb received a call from his office, informing him about an emergency at the rescue site. It was imperative for Najeeb to reach there as soon as possible.

"Sorry, girls, but I have to go. Duty calls—otherwise, I would have loved to make *qahwa* for all of you. Maybe next time. Also, I could be stuck at my office for a while, so please do not get all worked up, but I'm just a call away," he reminded them, shooting a quick glance at Gul. With that, he grabbed his phone, wallet, and the photograph and left the house.

With dinner cleared up, the girls resumed their work, each busy with their tasks. However, Gul realized that she couldn't find her notebook. She searched everywhere—under the table, behind the cushions—but couldn't locate it. Worried, she began rummaging through her purse, but it wasn't there either.

"Where did I put it? It's always in my purse when I'm not using it," she exclaimed in frustration, almost on the verge of tears.

Palwasha suggested Gul check the bedroom.

"Yes, I think I will," Gul replied, a bit exasperated. She knew these delays were putting them behind schedule. The notebook was important as it contained the names and contact numbers of all the vendors they were getting their materials from. "Oh bother," she scolded herself and hurried upstairs, taking the steps two at a time. Entering the bedroom, Gul searched through her desk drawers, almost emptying them out. She looked in the dresser drawers but found nothing. Now, she was really worried.

Where is it? I hope I didn't drop it when we went shopping for the materials. She panicked at the thought.

Standing in the middle of her room, she tried to think of all the places she might have put her diary.

Calm down, Gul, and think, she said to herself, attempting to curb her anxiety. "I have to retrace my steps in my mind. Only then will I be able to think more clearly."

She closed her eyes and took a deep breath and was exhaling slowly when suddenly, from the corner of her eye, she noticed something yellow sticking out of Palwasha's duffel bag on the window bench. It looked familiar. Looking at it more closely, she realized it was the same yellow bag that the girl had dumped on her in the parking lot. She had taken it to the guesthouse, intending to talk to Palwasha about it, but they had been so busy with everything else. Gul quickly moved toward the window, pulling the bag down from the bench. "Yes, that's the same bag." Looking through it, she saw her notebook. She had left her notebook inside the bag with the dress.

She sighed in relief.

Just as she was about to turn away, Gul noticed a folded piece of paper on the floor where she had placed Palwasha's bag. Thinking it might have fallen from her notebook, she unfolded it and quickly read what was written. At first, she couldn't fully comprehend the meaning of the note, so she read it again, her heart beating fast. Looking around nervously, she put the note in her shirt pocket, clutched her notebook tightly, and went downstairs. The girls were still busy, and the first dress was starting to take shape.

"Did you find your notebook?" Palwasha asked without looking up from her cutting board.

Gul, still lost in her thoughts about the note, simply nodded and returned to her seat.

"You don't look happy about it," Palwasha observed, pausing to look at her sister. "You look like you've seen a ghost." She chuckled.

Gul forced a smile, shaking her head. "No, no, I was just doing some mental calculations." She quickly made up an excuse. With that, she resumed her work with the accounting book and calculator, trying to focus on the task at hand.

An hour had passed, and everyone was engrossed in their work. Palwasha finally heaved a sigh of relief, her eyes scanning her creation from every angle with a critical eye. "Thank God," she exclaimed, straightening the collar of the jacket on the mannequin. "The cuts are good—just as I had sketched. Well, that's it for now. We'll do the stitching tomorrow," she announced, flexing and extending her fingers to relieve the stiffness, beaming at the two girls with satisfaction.

Gul, who had been focused on the accounting book, looked up and smiled. "You've truly poured your heart and soul into this, and I'm certain everything will turn out beautiful and elegant," she commented, gazing affectionately at her sister.

For a few moments, there was complete silence as the two sisters locked eyes.

"Look, Gul—" Palwasha began, but Gul interrupted her.

"I'm sorry, Palwasha." They both started at the same time and then stopped, realizing their simultaneous attempt to speak.

"Sorry, go ahead," both of them started again, causing them to burst into laughter.

Zarmeena, who had been quietly working at the cutting board, took the opportunity to slip out of the room, giving the sisters some space to resolve their issues. Palwasha walked up to her sister and sat on the coffee table, facing her with earnestness in her eyes.

"Gul, I'm sorry I didn't tell you about the photo shoot," she began, trying to mend the rift between them, "but believe me, there's nothing wrong with it. It's not out of line or anything like that. Nothing Ma or Ba wouldn't be okay with." Her eyes were shining with excitement. Gul listened attentively, refraining from interrupting as she saw Palwasha's genuine effort to explain. "You know, Gul, I wanted to raise the money for the workshop myself, and with the upcoming exhibition, I needed it quickly. I wanted to tell you, but you were busy with your exams, and I didn't want to bother you at the time. And…I didn't want to borrow money from Baba. In fact, I was planning to tell him about the photoshoot when he returned." Palwasha leaned back, a tad out of breath, anxiously awaiting Gul's response. Gul studied her sister intently, seeing the passion in her eyes for the work she was doing. She felt a pang of guilt for doubting Palwasha's judgment. Whatever she was planning must have been for a good reason. Gul regretted ever questioning her sister.

"Palwasha, I'm sorry. I should have talked to you first, and you're right—it's your project, and you know best how to handle it. I was just being overprotective—that's all," she apologized, sitting in front of her sister, holding her hand, "and you're right. I've been reviewing the payment orders and we definitely need more funds, especially with the exhibition approaching. We really do need to arrange more money." Gul opened her notebook to show Palwasha the rough calculations she had been working on when a folded piece of paper slipped from between the pages and fell onto the carpet. Palwasha caught it.

"Here, take this. It fell out of the notebook." She held the note with a somber expression.

Gul glanced at her sister and pushed the note back toward her. "It's not mine, Palwasha, but go ahead—take a look."

Puzzled, Palwasha took the note, following her sister's instruction. She unfolded it and scanned its contents. At first, it didn't make any sense to her, and she looked at Gul in confusion. "What is this? Some kind of joke?" she asked, rereading the note out loud: *"Please help?"*

Palwasha's curiosity grew, and she questioned her sister, "Gul, what's going on? Who needs help, and where did you get this note?"

Leaning forward, Gul replied, "Palwasha, I found it in your duffel bag when I went upstairs to look for my notebook."

Palwasha was taken aback. "In my bag? But I don't understand what this note was doing in my bag and how your notebook ended up there!" She examined the note once again. Puzzled, she focused on the letter *F* at the bottom. "This is really strange, and who would write such a note, and why is it signed with the letter *F*? She looked at it even more closely. "And whose name starts with an *F*?" she questioned, trying to rack her brains, thinking of all her family and friends. Suddenly, with a look of incredulous surprise, a whisper came out of her mouth. "*Farah*? But why in the world would she write such a note? I've never seen this note before." She was genuinely confused, looking at her sister for some kind of clarity.

"Yes…it's Farah. I'm sure," Gul replied, taking the note back and putting it carefully in her purse.

"But why would she write such a strange note and put it in my bag? I hardly know her. And what type of trouble is she in that she resorted to such cloak-and-dagger antics? If something was wrong, she could have gone straight to the authorities, no?" Palwasha was worked up.

Gul took a deep breath, trying to gather her thoughts. "Palwasha, I'm genuinely concerned about your safety," she explained, her voice filled with worry. "We should show this note to Najeeb. He's in a better position to assess the situation and guide us on what to do next." Gul still hadn't revealed everything to Palwasha, but she knew it was important to warn her sister first.

Palwasha shook her head, still not convinced. "But, Gul, I have to go and get my payments from Farah. I can't just let it go because of a strange note!"

Throwing up her hands in the air, Gul's frustration was at its peak. But she knew that once Palwasha made up her mind, it was difficult to change it. Reluctantly, Gul agreed, nodding slowly. "Okay but you're going on one condition: I'm coming with you," she declared.

"That's more like my sister. I never thought that you'd say that," Palwasha cried out in excitement. "And, Gul, note or no note, I was planning to go for the next photo shoot anyway just so you know," she added with a mischievous grin. Gul knew that her sister's determination couldn't be easily curbed.

Playfully, she threw a cushion at Palwasha. "And here we thought we had you tamed."

Palwasha laughed and dodged the cushion, causing it to knock over a bowl of popcorn onto the floor. "Oh, look, Gul, what have you done?" She pointed at the mess, pretending to be angry. "Let me clean the mess. The whole room looks like it was hit by a tornado." With that, she grabbed a broom and dustpan. The atmosphere in the room was transformed; the girls were engaged in a light hearted banter, tidying up the fabric that was strewn around, pushing the furniture back in their original place.

"Palwasha, I have a feeling that something is not right at the guesthouse and Farah specifically asked for *your* help," Gul expressed. "It's obvious that she put the note in your bag during the photo shoot. Everyone knows Najeeb's position and our family, yet she still chose you to ask for help discreetly. Don't you think it's a bit strange?"

Palwasha, feeling exhausted, sat back on the sofa and looked at Gul, trying to grasp her sister's point. "What exactly are you trying to say, Gul? I don't get it," she asked, feeling a bit flustered.

"My point is that although we know she is the owner of the guesthouse, she still has to resort to this suspicious behavior. She can't just openly ask anybody for help, and that could only mean she is under some kind of duress!" Gul stated, her eyes shining. She looked at her sister, who was almost lying on the sofa, stretching her arms up in the air.

"That means she's in some kind of trouble," Palwasha asked, trying to suppress a yawn, her mind a bit foggy trying to make sense of all the strange going-ons.

"My point exactly! That's why, Palwasha, we have to tell Najeeb about the note. He will definitely know what to do," Gul explained, bothered by the whole situation. She knew that whatever was needed to be done would have to wait until morning when Najeeb returned from the office.

"When is Najeeb coming back?" Palwasha asked, her eyes hurting from the lack of sleep. She had been working nonstop for quite a few hours on the design board, and at this point, she desperately wanted to crawl into bed and shut her mind.

"No idea, but I think because of the emergency situation, he won't be back anytime tonight." Gul turned off the light. "Come on, get up, Palwasha. Let's turn in," Gul urged her sister, holding out her hand.

Palwasha gave a lopsided smile. "You know, the best days were when we used to pretend to be asleep, and Baba used to carry us upstairs to our bed. I used to do that on purpose," Palwasha reminisced.

Getting up, the sisters locked the doors and went upstairs to their bedroom.

CHAPTER 19

The Chase

"Zarmeena must be asleep by now. It's pretty quiet," Palwasha observed, opening the door slowly so as not to wake their cousin. To their surprise, the bedside table lamp was on, but Zarmeena was nowhere to be found.

"Oh, she is not here?" Palwasha looked around, feeling the start of a headache.

"She must be sleeping in the guestroom, but I wonder why?" Gul replied. Gul trudged into the dressing room to change into her night clothes. As she was about to close the door, Palwasha, who had gone to the guestroom to call Zarmeena, stood in the doorway, looking somewhat annoyed.

"Gul! Zarmeena is not in the guestroom," Palwasha informed, a puzzled expression on her face.

"Well, she must be downstairs," Gul speculated, trying to make Palwasha move so that she could change.

"No, I already checked. She isn't in the house. I looked downstairs as well," Palwasha insisted, still standing her ground.

"What? Not in the house?" Gul repeated. She checked her wristwatch, which showed it was way past midnight. "She must have gone out for a walk then." Gul felt a bit worried now. "Call her on her cellphone, and in the meantime, we can go out and check. She might have dozed off on one of the recliners on the veranda." It was unlike Zarmeena to be sitting alone somewhere for such a long time.

Palwasha tried calling Zarmeena's number, but the line wouldn't connect. "The connection is so bad during the night here in the valley it's impossible to contact anyone in the first go," she complained.

Both girls hurried downstairs, calling out for their cousin, but she was nowhere to be found. They looked everywhere in the house, but there was no response. They quickly unlocked the door, hoping to find Zarmeena on the veranda, but to their surprise, it was deserted. Puzzled, Palwasha tried calling her cousin again. The line had connected, but this time, there was no reply. She tried again, but still received no answer. Worried, she looked at her sister. "No answer." Her voice was worrisome.

At this point, the girls were outside in the backyard, but there was no sign of their cousin. "Just keep trying her number," Gul instructed. "In the meantime, let me go around the house to check the garage!" Palwasha remained in the front lawn, continuously attempting to call Zarmeena, but without success. The fatigue she had felt earlier had now transformed into worry for her cousin. It was unlike Zarmeena to disappear without informing them. Palwasha glanced at her cellphone. It showed "Ringing," but there was no response from the other end.

"Pick up, Zarmeena, pick up," Palwasha urged, looking around the moonlit grounds, surrounded by shadows. The full moon shone brightly, and Palwasha's mind wandered to thoughts of werewolves and the possibility that Zarmeena had been taken by one.

What's wrong with me? she muttered, annoyed at her own train of thought.

She looked at the pathway leading back to the garage and the driveway, wondering where Gul had gone. Restlessness began to consume Palwasha, and she regretted not going with her sister. She paced back and forth in the lawn, feeling a sense of urgency. She tried calling Zarmeena's number once again, but instead of a response, she thought she could hear the distant ringing of a phone. The sound seemed to be coming from somewhere on the sidewalk. The phone continued to ring, and the sound grew louder. Almost instinctively, Palwasha ran around the house towards the driveway, following the source of the ringing.

"Thank God, Zarmeena! Where have you been? We've been worried sick!" Palwasha shouted, her phone still connected and the ringtone growing louder. However, her relief quickly turned into confusion when she saw Gul approaching her, holding a phone that was continuously ringing. Palwasha glanced at her own cell, disconnected the call, and the ringing immediately stopped. The phone in Gul's hand went silent. Fear was evident in Gul's eyes as she stood in front of Palwasha.

Palwasha almost snatched the phone from her sister's hand, her voice filled with surprise. Then she looked behind Gul and asked, "But where is Zarmeena?"

"I don't know! I found it in the rose bed near the garage," Gul whispered, her voice hoarse with worry. She looked pale as if she had seen a ghost. "But her car is here... Do you think she went down the trail?" The sudden cry of wolves made them jump, their hearts pounding as they looked around, filled with fear.

"Gul, she could be lying hurt somewhere. How will we be able to look for her? We can't search the thicket before dawn!" Palwasha was on the verge of tears.

By now, they had retreated to the safety of the veranda, sitting on the steps. Palwasha glanced at her sister, but Gul remained silent. Then Palwasha pulled out her phone and tried calling Najeeb, but the call wouldn't go through. She looked at Gul with desperation.

"I don't know where he is, but the call is not going through," Palwasha said, feeling helpless.

As they were contemplating their next move when out of nowhere, they heard a car engine start; the sound was coming from the driveway. Without warning, Gul made a dash for the driveway with Palwasha following closely behind—both of their hearts pounding. They swiftly crossed the lawn, heading toward the driveway where the cars were parked. To their utter astonishment, they saw the taillights of Zarmeena's car as it turned onto the main road and vanished into the darkness.

"What the heck? Zarmeena! Zarmeena!" Gul exclaimed at the top of her voice. Thinking quickly, she turned to her sister. "Palwasha, quickly grab the car keys!" But Palwasha was already a step ahead, rushing back inside to retrieve the keys. And within minutes, they were in their car and driving down the main road, chasing after Zarmeena's car.

"Turn right! Turn right at the next traffic light," Gul directed her sister, gripping the dashboard tightly. As they made the turn, they caught a glimpse of distant taillights ahead, but they had no way of knowing if it was Zarmeena's car. The car ahead was gradually moving farther and farther away, and Palwasha was determined not to lose sight of it. Throwing caution to the wind, she pressed hard on the gas pedal. Eventually, they caught up to the car, but upon closer inspection, their hopes deflated. It was some other car, not Zarmeena's—and the girls were now panicking.

"*Where did the car disappear?*" Palwasha shouted in frustration, her voice echoing in the night. "And why would Zarmeena be running away from us?" Palwasha detested this game of cat and mouse, especially under the cover of darkness. "What is going on?" she asked her sister, her mind spinning with questions. "There is only one road from our house up to the fountain roundabout. How did we catch up to that other car and not see Zarmeena's car? This doesn't make sense at all." Palwasha's thoughts continued to race. She made a U-turn at the next traffic light, heading back toward their house, determined to find answers. Suddenly, Gul slammed her hand on the dashboard, startling Palwasha.

"I know, Palwasha! This is the only main road up to the roundabout, but remember, there is another dirt road that branches off from the main road just before we cross the bridge. It's a narrow trail, not meant for regular traffic. Let's go check that!" Gul exclaimed with a mix of urgency and hope.

Palwasha nodded, willing to try any option at this point. Without wasting a moment, Palwasha made another sharp turn and steered the car back toward the bridge. As they approached the turn leading into the thicket, the girls held their breath. Palwasha maneuvered the car onto the bumpy dirt track, and the surroundings enveloped them in darkness with only the headlights piercing through the thick gloom. The eerie silence hung heavy in the air, heightening their fear and anticipation. Suddenly, the silence was shattered by Gul's piercing scream. Palwasha slammed her foot on the brake pedal, bringing the car to a screeching halt. For a second, the animal's mesmerizing marble-like eyes remained fixed in a stare, and then as suddenly as it had appeared, it trotted off into the darkness.

Gul's heart raced.

"We almost killed it!" Her hands braced against the dashboard; she took a moment to catch her breath. She turned to her sister, who was now frowning at her in disapproval.

"No, Gul. *You* almost gave me a heart attack!" Palwasha shouted. She gripped the steering wheel tightly. "I know where I'm going. Next time, try to express your fear without startling me!" She shook her head, still reeling from the surge of panic. "Please don't ever do that again. We were just inches away from hitting that big boulder." Gul looked ahead and saw the looming rock, realizing just how close they had come to disaster. She let out a sigh of relief.

"Sorry, Palwasha. I'm just feeling so on edge." Gul's worry about the situation weighed heavily on her mind. They had impulsively followed a trail of uncertainty, unsure of what they would find. Her thoughts turned to Zarmeena, her worry for her cousin consuming her thoughts. Zarmeena's sudden disappearance without a word was completely out of character.

The girls continued along the dusty road, feeling the car jolt and bounce on the uneven gravel track, uncertain of where this unknown path would lead them.

"I really don't know where this track will take us," Palwasha expressed her skepticism. The dark road stretched ahead like an endless slithering snake in the middle of nowhere. Gul and Palwasha started to doubt their decision, feeling as though they were embarking on a fruitless pursuit. Palwasha glanced at the rearview mirror and quickly averted her gaze. The darkness behind them felt ominous, adding to their growing unease. After driving for nearly fifteen minutes, Palwasha became increasingly convinced that they had lost their way.

"Gul, I don't think we're on the right path," she finally voiced her fears. But before Gul could respond, they reached an opening in the road, revealing the guesthouse bathed in moonlight across the clearing of the cul-de-sac. The car slowed almost to a stop as they took in the sight before them. Both sisters sat in silence, their faces reflecting astonishment. It was not a surprise yet unexpected at the same time.

"Oh my! Now what?" Palwasha commented, her gaze fixed on the imposing iron gates that stood before them. They had no way of knowing if it was safe to cross the iron fence, and the memory of the fierce-looking dogs they had seen during the photo shoots at the guesthouse flashed through Palwasha's mind. She chewed on her lower lip, contemplating the connection between their cousin and the guesthouse.

How were they supposed to gain entry?

"Palwasha!" Gul smacked her sister on the arm, breaking her train of thought. "I'm talking to you. Snap out of it!"

"Listen, Palwasha, circle the cul-de-sac slowly," Gul directed her sister. "I'm pretty sure there's a small dirt track at the back of the guesthouse." Gul felt confident about the track, though she kept her fingers crossed, hoping to find Zarmeena as soon as possible. Palwasha looked at her sister with a surprised expression, tilting her head to one side.

"You seem to know a lot about this location." She gave Gul a knowing smile. Putting the car in gear, Palwasha circled the cul-de-sac slowly, keeping a sharp lookout for the hidden track. Suddenly, she exclaimed, "Look, Gul! There it is!" Her excitement grew as they spotted an opening branching off the cul-de-sac, hidden by overgrown bushes but wide enough for a car or even a lorry to pass through. Gul shared in the excitement, acknowledging her knowledge of the location.

"I guess I was right, and yes, I do know the area thanks to all the hiking and biking I've done with Zarmeena in our spare time," Gul explained, shooting a side glance at her sister. Memories of the weekends they had spent together, excluding Palwasha due to her unavailability, crossed Gul's mind. Palwasha shifted uncomfortably in her seat, aware of the implied remark, but she chose to remain silent. Carefully maneuvering the car along the dirt track, which was covered by overgrown trees forming a natural tunnel, Palwasha decided to stop. Just as she was about to turn off the headlights, she hit the brakes abruptly and stared ahead. Both girls could see the silhouette of a car in the distance.

But whose car was it?

Palwasha continued to gaze at the hidden car, covered by a tarp, making it difficult to determine the type and model. Carefully, Palwasha parked her car next to the covered vehicle, turning off the engine and the lights. She turned to her sister and asked, "So what's our next step? There's no sign of Zarmeena's car, and that car seems to belong to someone who rarely uses it, given that it's covered." Palwasha felt certain they had embarked on a wild goose chase. She quickly dismissed the idea that Zarmeena might have gone to her own place, knowing it was highly unlikely. With a resigned sigh, Palwasha tapped her sister on the shoulder and asked, "Any more bright ideas about what to do next?"

Gul nodded, looking back, "Let's explore the back side and see if we can find a way onto the grounds. There might be a broken fence or something." She quickly unbuckled her seatbelt and stepped out of the car, motioning for her sister to do the same. Palwasha nodded and hurriedly got out of the car. However, Gul started tiptoeing in the opposite direction.

Confused, Palwasha ran up to her sister and whispered in a slightly annoyed tone, "Gul, what are you doing? We're supposed to be heading towards the grounds." She wasn't sure what Gul had in mind.

Without answering, Gul moved toward the covered car and whispered back, "I just want to check something just to be sure," crouching against the covered car. Palwasha followed suit; it was best to follow her sister's lead rather than ask more questions. Gul suddenly stopped and carefully pulled one corner of the tarp from the back side, which was loosely tied, revealing the back of the car.

In the dim light, Palwasha strained to read the number plate: "GLT 242." Eye squinting, Palwasha slowly made out the number as her voice slowly filled with disbelief. "GLT 242! Oh my god, Gul, that's Zarmeena's car!" she reiterated.

CHAPTER 20

The Missing Link

The two girls remained crouched by the car, their minds racing as they contemplated ways to enter the building and search for Zarmeena. Gul tried to connect the dots, but so far, she was drawing a blank. She was worried for her cousin and for themselves. She did not know what they were getting into, but one thing was certain: Something fishy was going on behind those walls, and they had to find Zarmeena. She turned to her sister, who by the look on her face was trying to make sense of all the happenings.

Taking a deep breath, Gul squeezed her sister's hand, attempting to sound more confident than she felt. "Finding Zarmeena's car here means she's around here somewhere. Before we try to get inside the building ourselves, I'll try to call Najeeb and tell him about everything that has happened." Gul took out her phone and dialed Najeeb's number, but an automated voice message informed her about the unavailability of mobile phone service. Frustrated, Gul put the phone away. "Nothing seems to be going right, and where is Najeeb when we need him? He's not available!" she exclaimed, her voice filled with frustration.

Palwasha gave her a slight nudge. "Listen, Gul, he must be busy and unable to receive our calls. But we can't just sit here and do nothing. We have to find Zarmeena." Tears welled up in her eyes. "I feel like this is all my fault. I've dragged you and Zarmeena into this mess. I'm sorry."

Gul moved closer to Palwasha, clasping her hands. "Look, it's not your fault that Zarmeena is missing," Gul reassured her. "Come, let's pull the tarp back down in place just in case," Gul nudged her sister into action. Palwasha nodded, a bit relieved, and helped her sister tie the tarp the way it was before, ensuring that nothing appeared out of the ordinary.

"Gul, I was thinking, instead of trying to cross the grounds, why don't we check if any of the windows towards the back side are unlocked? That way, we could directly enter the building," Palwasha suggested. Gul agreed, thinking it was a much better plan than attempting to navigate the front lawn. They moved quickly, checking the windows one by one at the back of the building. At the fourth window, Gul got lucky. Carefully, she pulled on the window, and it opened silently without any resistance. Her heart skipped a beat, grateful for the fortunate break.

"Palwasha, help me get in," Gul whispered. But there was no response. "Palwasha!" she called out again, this time in a louder whisper. Nervously, she glanced back and saw her sister crouching beside Zarmeena's car. Surprised, Gul called out once more, "Palwasha, what are you doing? Come and help me get in." She wondered what her sister was thinking.

Palwasha looked up and motioned for her to be quiet. Then she quickly loosened the air valves of all four tires of Zarmeena's car. Gul chuckled as she realized her sister's plan. Time was of the essence, and they knew they had to act swiftly before dawn broke, making it more challenging to find Zarmeena.

"Hurry up, Palwasha," Gul insisted, waiting for her sister near the window.

Palwasha joined her, slightly out of breath. "Whoever took Zarmeena and her car won't be leaving in a hurry," Palwasha remarked, a satisfied smile playing at the corner of her mouth.

Gul gave a small chuckle. "I hope Zarmeena won't mind, but first we have to find her…and quickly." Gul motioned for her sister to come and help her over the window ledge. "Palwasha, this one is open. Just give me a push so I can climb over," Gul explained. Palwasha nodded and braced herself against the wall, interlocking her fingers to create a foothold for Gul. Carefully, Gul placed her foot on Palwasha's interlocked hands, holding onto the window ledge, which was almost five feet high from the ground. "Okay, hold steady, Palwasha, and on the count of three, give me a heave up with all your strength," Gul directed.

Palwasha nodded, positioning her feet apart to maintain balance. On the count of three, she pushed her sister up with all her might. Gul let out a groan and pulled herself up over the ledge. With a bit of effort, she climbed inside the dark room illuminated only by moonlight. Gul stood still for a moment, making sure there was no one there. She realized it was some kind of pantry.

Good, otherwise I could have landed in someone's bedroom, and that wouldn't have been good.

The thought made her chuckle. Looking around for something to help Palwasha climb up through the window, Gul found a storage area with dining linens. She quickly took a couple of table covers, tied the ends, and secured one end to the leg of a heavy wooden table. She threw the other end out of the window.

"Palwasha, take the end and try to pull yourself up," Gul softly called. Palwasha, who had been waiting quietly, worried for Gul's safety, grabbed onto the cloth and successfully climbed inside with Gul pulling on the other end.

"Gosh, that was hard," Palwasha groaned, a bit out of breath. She looked around, rubbing her grazed palms. "Next time, I'll throw the line to you, and you can climb in like I did," she whispered. Gul motioned for her to be quiet and tiptoed toward the door, signaling for her sister to follow. Slowly and cautiously, Gul turned the doorknob and peered outside. They found themselves in the section of the guesthouse designated for staff, including the kitchen, storage rooms, and laundry area. The hallway was dimly lit, devoid of any people. Gul closed the door and turned to her sister, who was standing against the wall.

"Well?" Palwasha asked.

"Well," Gul mimicked her sister, "it looks like we're in the kitchen and dining area or something similar, but I have no idea where to look for Zarmeena." Gul expressed her confusion, looking at her sister helplessly.

Palwasha snapped her fingers in front of Gul's face to get her attention. "Let's find Farah first, and I'm sure she'll lead us to Zarmeena."

Gul smiled at her sister, feeling a glimmer of hope. However, her expression quickly changed to disappointment. "But where are Farah's quarters? We can't just wander around the guesthouse knocking on every door in search of her room." Ignoring her comment, Palwasha slipped past her and ventured out into the hallway.

"Palwasha! Palwasha! Have you lost your mind!?" She whispered loudly, trying to keep her voice down. Gul looked up and down the hallway before tiptoeing her way to where Palwasha was standing, worried Palwasha would get them caught.

Palwasha pointed toward a door with a porthole window. "There are uniforms in there," Palwasha whispered excitedly.

Gul was completely bewildered. "Clearly, Palwasha, you're not thinking straight. Why are you so interested in uniforms when we're trying to find Farah's room?"

"The uniforms for the guesthouse staff, idiot." She rolled her eyes. Without wasting any more time explaining to her sister, she pushed open the door and went straight into the room. The room had shelves attached to the walls, stacked with clean linen, towels, laundry materials, toiletries, and along one wall, there were neatly stacked black and white usher's uniforms. Palwasha quickly grabbed two uniforms off the shelf, throwing one in Gul's direction. "We need to change into these in case we bump into anyone," she urged. Palwasha swiftly put on the coat over her shirt and did the same with the trousers. "Hurry up, Gul," she encouraged her sister, noticing Gul's hesitation. "Just put it on over your shirt, and let's move." Palwasha helped Gul with the buttons of the coat.

"Well, I think I've instantly gained a pound or two," Gul remarked, trying to adjust the collar of her shirt. "I feel so stuffed wearing two layers of clothes like this." She looked up and saw her sister buttoning up her shirt, and she couldn't help but giggle.

"What is it now?" Palwasha asked, a bit annoyed.

"Oh, nothing. It's just funny. You look the part with your hair tucked in the hat, but nobody's giving you a modeling job anytime soon with that stuffed belly," Gul teased, patting the layers of clothing Palwasha was wearing.

"Well, thank you for nothing," Palwasha retorted, making a face at her sister, "and yes, listen, just follow me. I once overheard Farah mention that her quarters were on the third floor." She adjusted her cap. With that, she slipped out of the room, Gul following closely behind.

The girls found themselves in a hallway that opened up into an atrium, connecting the main corridor to the lobby and two other paths leading to the back patio and the area where they had entered from. Bathed in the soft glow of the wall sconces, they took a moment to survey their surroundings.

"There it is," Palwasha whispered, pointing toward the elevator.

However, Gul stopped her, realizing the potential risks. "Using the elevator might attract attention. We need to find another way," she advised. Palwasha nodded, acknowledging the wisdom in her sister's words. Just as she was about to look for an alternative, Gul spotted the emergency exit staircase door tucked away next to a large potted plant, offering a more discreet option. A sense of relief washed over Palwasha. Thinking that her sister's keen observation skills had come in handy, Palwasha felt grateful for Gul's attentiveness.

"The door is locked," Gul said hopelessly.

With no other option, Palwasha moved toward the elevator, drawn to the numbers displayed above the elevator door. She noticed that it only went up to the second floor, which struck her as odd.

"Somebody at the photo shoot mentioned getting things from Farah's quarter on the third floor. But this only goes to the second. This elevator is of no use." There was a sinking feeling in her stomach.

As the sisters stood in the stillness of the night, contemplating their next move, the silence was shattered by the sudden echoing sound of footsteps descending from the main lobby area. The girls froze, fear gripping their hearts as the footsteps grew closer and louder.

Thinking quickly, Gul pulled Palwasha to the side, concealing themselves behind a large planter near the exit door. They held their breath, mentally prepared to pounce on the stranger if he approached. Gul strained to listen to the oncoming footsteps, desperately hoping their presence had gone unnoticed.

Then the footsteps stopped.

Palwasha tightened her grip on her sister's arm, holding her breath, wondering anxiously if they had been discovered. In the shadowy recess where the sisters were hiding, both of them strained their eyes, barely able to see the silhouette of a figure. The man had stopped abruptly in front of a seemingly solid wall. To their astonishment, a panel on the wall slid open noiselessly, revealing a hidden elevator. A man let out a sigh of relief and stepped inside, disappearing as the door closed behind him.

Gul turned to her sister. "Did you see that?" Palwasha nodded, equally surprised by what they had just witnessed.

Now this is getting interesting, Palwasha thought.

Their adventure had taken an unexpected turn, revealing a secret passage within the guesthouse. Without wasting any time, Gul and Palwasha approached the wall panel where the elevator had emerged. Looking closely, they noticed a strange-looking keypad.

"Now what?" Gul remarked, exasperated. She shot a quick glance up and down the corridor, making sure the coast was clear.

Palwasha, who was standing right behind her sister, gave Gul a soft nudge, "This thing must have a code or something!"

"Shhh, let me think, Palwa," Gul whispered, examining the keypad, hoping to decipher its purpose. She tapped a few buttons experimentally, but nothing happened. The arrangement of numbers and symbols on the keypad were a bit strange. "I don't understand," Gul muttered, her brows furrowed in confusion, when her gaze fell upon a small plaque attached to the wall near the water fountain.

It bore a cryptic poem written in elegant calligraphy:

> Seek the *light* in darkness's embrace.
> Let the *symbols* guide your destined trace.
> Unlock the *path* to secrets untold,
> Where *truth* and deceit shall soon unfold.

Gul read the words under her breath, her voice filled with both anticipation and trepidation. She turned to her sister, a glimmer of excitement in her eyes. "Those words on the plaque...why put such a random plaque on a wall? And look at the italicized letters in each row. This must mean something!" Her excitement increased. "Palwasha, I think this is our clue." The girls carefully examined the plaque, studying the words etched upon it.

"But, Gul, this keypad is numerical, and the verse has only letters."

The girls felt stumped.

Palwasha shook her head. "This is just a dumb idea. We're just wasting time!"

But Gul had zoned out Palwasha's ranting and was looking at the words on the plaque with a strange expression.

"Maybe the italic words represent a number?" she mumbled to herself. "Yes! That's it!" Her excitement was palpable.

A bit taken aback, Palwasha looked at her sister. "What do you mean?"

"Lights, symbols, path, truth. It's their placement in the line!" Gul repeated the words.

"Three...three...three...two," Palwasha mouthed, moving forward as she carefully tapped the keypad.

Both the girls held their breath, but nothing happened.

"Wait. Try 5...7...4...5," Gul whispered, still staring at the plaque.

Without hesitation, Palwasha entered the numbers. It formed a perfect triangular shape on the keypad. To their astonishment, the panel on the wall slid open, revealing an elevator.

Gul released a sharp exhale and stepped inside, glancing at her sister with a sense of trepidation. "It was the number of letters in each word." She sighed in relief.

"Well, I suppose we're on the right track. Let's just hope we don't encounter a welcoming party on the other side," Palwasha whispered, crossing her fingers and silently praying for their safety.

Gul pressed the button for the third floor, and within seconds, the elevator came to a stop. The doors slid open, and the girls again held their breath, uncertain of what awaited them on the other side. The area seems to be deserted. Without wasting any time, they stepped out of the elevator. Cautiously surveying their surroundings, they noticed a sitting area with several sofas. Palwasha motioned Gul to follow her in that direction. Hastily, the sisters positioned themselves behind the largest sofa, crouching low against it. The corridor was illuminated by soft night lights, boasting an ethereal glow.

"Why are we hiding here?" Gul whispered, peeking from behind the couch. "Did you see anybody?"

"No, no. I just didn't want to take the chance. The person we saw is supposedly on this floor, remember?"

After a few minutes of waiting, Palwasha motioned for them to get up. "Okay, the coast is clear, and Farah's room is 309—if I remember correctly," Palwasha whispered, peering out cautiously from behind the sofa, her eyes glued to the corridor.

"Room 309," Gul repeated, surprised. "I didn't know you were that friendly with Farah for her to tell you the room number." Gul's tone carried a hint of jealousy. Palwasha chuckled softly, shaking her head.

Both the girls then crept down the corridor, checking the numbers on the doors until they finally reached room 309.

"Here goes nothing," Palwasha let out.

Just as Palwasha was about to touch the doorknob, they heard the key turning in the lock. Panic surged through Palwasha, freezing her in place. Gul grabbed her sister's hand and swiftly pulled them both into a niche next to the door, conveniently hidden by a nearby water fountain. They held their breath, hoping whoever was inside wouldn't notice their presence. The door opened, and they heard a man's voice talking angrily to someone inside the room.

"You better!" the man shrieked as he walked out of the room, lighting a cigarette.

The girls were frozen, hands clasped to their mouths, filled with fear. They listened as the door closed followed by the sound of the key turning in the lock echoed in the corridor, and the footsteps receded in the opposite direction. The sisters remained motionless, not daring to make a sound. After a couple of minutes, Palwasha cautiously peered out from the shadows. The corridor was empty, devoid of any sign of the man who had emerged from the room. Gul craned her neck to look at the door. Her heart started beating faster, and she clutched Palwasha's hand tightly.

"Gul, what's the matter?" Palwasha retorted in a hushed tone.

"The key!" Gul exclaimed, her excitement mounting. Without hesitation, she stepped out from the shadows and turned the key in the lock. As luck would have it, the man had left the key in the lock.

"Luck seems to be on our side tonight," Palwasha whispered, pleasantly surprised.

"Shhhh." Gul motioned for her to keep quiet.

With trembling fingers, Gul slowly turned the doorknob; the door opened noiselessly. She peered inside, taking her time to assess the situation. Palwasha breathed down her neck, urging her to move, fearful that the man might return at any moment. The room was engulfed in complete darkness as the girls stepped in cautiously, closing the door softly behind them. Their eyes strained to adjust to the dim surroundings. Palwasha gripped her sister's arm firmly, ready to pull her back at the slightest hint of danger. A faint whimpering sound emanated from the far corner of the suite, causing the girls to freeze in their tracks. Gul, who was leading the way, could make out a huddled figure behind the desk on the floor near an overturned chair. Palwasha reached into her coat pocket, searching for her mobile phone. Switching it on, she activated the flashlight and directed its beam towards the source of the sound. She gasped in astonishment, finding it hard to believe what she saw before her.

"*Farah?*" Palwasha called out, her voice trembling with both surprise and concern. Looking confused, Palwasha whispered, "Farah, what happened?" She moved past her sister, almost stumbling over the overturned chair.

Farah's face was streaked with tears, her hands and feet tied with duct tape plastered across her mouth. She couldn't register who was calling out her name, but when she saw the two girls, the fear in her eyes transformed into confusion and then utter disbelief. Looking around, Gul hastily switched on the desk lamp, illuminating the room. The girls could see that Farah had a few bruises on her face.

A look of horror appeared on Palwasha's face as she tried to help Farah sit up straight, hands trembling. Gul stood there, frozen; the sharp contrast between the confident and suave woman she had first encountered compared to the timid figure she saw lying before her left Gul in disbelief. As Palwasha tended to Farah, Gul couldn't help but wonder about the identity of Farah's tormentor.

Stepping out of the shadows, Gul questioned softly, "Who did this to you?" Farah's attention had been solely on Palwasha as she untied her hands and feet, carefully removing the duct tape. Startled, Farah's gaze shifted toward Gul, confusion etched across her face. Her eyes darted back and forth between Palwasha and Gul.

"Keep still, Farah," Palwasha ordered as she carefully removed the tape from Farah's mouth, which felt like a burning rash on her skin. Farah nodded, looking at Palwasha with questioning eyes. Palwasha noticed the look and sat back, gesturing toward Gul. "Farah, this is my twin sister, Gul." Palwasha introduced her sister to the woman. Farah, still in shock, simply nodded slowly, struggling to process this new information. Clearing her throat and searching for the right words, Gul looked at Farah with a determined expression.

But before Gul could say anything, Farah asked the first question: "How come you girls are here?" Farah rubbed her wrists where the ropes had cut into her skin.

The sisters exchanged glances, unsure of whether they could fully trust Farah. Even though she was found tied up and helpless on the floor, they couldn't dismiss the possibility that she had some connection to Zarmeena's disappearance.

Sensing their hesitation, Farah took a deep breath and addressed the sisters, looking intently. "Listen, girls, I need your help." Her voice was wavering, almost pleading. Trying to push herself to stand up, she cried out in pain, collapsing back into the chair. She groaned in agony, sweat glistening on her furrowed brow. With dismay in her eyes, she looked at the girls and uttered, "My ankle...I think I twisted it."

It looks like a sprain. How will she be able to walk, let alone stand? Gul's mind raced with thoughts.

They had come to find Zarmeena, but instead, they found Farah with a sprained ankle. Gul's heart sank as she felt the weight of the situation.

While Gul was lost in thought, Palwasha was engaged in conversation with Farah, trying to uncover the circumstances that led to her helpless state.

Palwasha cried out in astonishment. "What are you saying, Farah? That man was the guesthouse manager?" She glanced at her sister in shock.

Gul maintained her composure, refusing to display any emotion. Deep down, she knew that the person behind this act was dangerous. Time was running out, and finding Zarmeena before dawn became even more crucial. Studying Farah intently, Gul stood with her hands folded across her chest.

"But tell me, Farah, why would the manager tie you up like that?" Gul's tone remained skeptical, and Farah could sense the underlying animosity. However, she chose to overlook it and turned her gaze toward Palwasha, her eyes welling up with tears in desperation.

Palwasha quickly stepped in. "Farah, calm down, please. We have to find our cousin Zarmeena, and we think she is somewhere here in the guesthouse."

Farah shook her head, not understanding. "I don't understand. You girls came looking for your cousin here? But why do you think she's here?" Farah paused, looking confused.

Palwasha clarified, "We believe she was kidnapped from our house. We followed her car, and it led us here."

Farah took in a sharp breath, blinking rapidly. "Oh, then you girls need to act fast. The girls have already left for the airport, and they might be in danger."

Palwasha's heart dropped upon hearing what Farah had to say. "The airport?" she repeated, a look of horror on her face. She glanced at her sister and could see the panic on Gul's face. Turning to Farah, she felt an overwhelming urge to shake the woman by her shoulders. "What does that mean? What other girls are you talking about?" Farah, wincing in pain, struggled to provide answers.

"The girls…the models left for the city this morning. Their flight to Dubai is scheduled for this evening. If your cousin is with them, then she is in trouble." Farah's face contorted in pain as she bent down, rubbing her swollen ankle.

Palwasha pulled Gul to a corner away from Farah's hearing range. "Listen, Gul, the models left in the morning. Zarmeena can't be with them because she was with us until a few hours ago."

Gul, keeping a close eye on Farah, nodded. She walked up to Farah with a stern expression, still suspicious of Farah's motives. "Why are you so worried about the girls going to Dubai?" Gul was seething with anger. "Give us a straight answer!"

Taken aback by the derision in Gul's tone, Farah very well knew that at that point she had no chance but to comply. She took in a deep breath. "The girls traveling to Dubai…they don't know it, but they're carrying stolen artifacts and smuggled jewels in their luggage. If they get caught, they'll be in a lot of trouble." Farah began to sob, looking helpless. "You have to get help—please!"

The sisters' hearts dropped at the predicament the unsuspecting girls would find themselves in if they were caught smuggling the goods. And now they themselves had unwittingly stumbled into a sinister smugglers' den.

"Listen, Gul, try calling Najeeb's number and inform him about the situation—this is really serious. We need his help now more than ever," Palwasha said in desperation.

Gul nodded, her hands sweaty. Gul took out her phone and attempted to call Najeeb, but the network failed every time. She felt flustered and looked at Palwasha with despair.

Thinking quickly, Palwasha turned to her sister. "Gul, it's no use getting both of us caught, and we cannot wait for Najeeb. Whatever we have to do, we need to do it ourselves. The manager might come back at any moment." She paused for a moment, shifting her weight to the other leg. "I will help you take Farah to the car, and I will backtrack and look for Zarmeena. We know she is here, and I know my way around here."

Palwasha had already anticipated her sister's response, but she still believed her idea was the best course of action.

Gul gave her sister a piercing look and took a step back. "No way." She shook her head firmly. "I am not leaving you here all alone."

Palwasha let out a sigh. "Okay then, help me support Farah. Let's get her out of here first, and then we can figure out our next move."

Gul nodded and approached Farah to assist her, making sure to support her on her good foot. Palwasha took a cautious step toward the door to see if the coast was clear. Slowly and carefully, she turned the doorknob and peered outside. Her throat went dry as she saw a man coming down the corridor. Her pulse quickened, and she silently closed the door, motioning for her sister and Farah to remain quiet. Frantically, Palwasha looked around and spotted the duct tape she had removed from Farah's face, which was now stuck to the side of the desk. With a quick movement, she ripped it off the surface and, without hesitation, placed it back across Farah's mouth. Taken aback, Farah tried to resist, groaning.

"Shh, shhh. Shut up!" Palwasha hissed. "Gul, hurry," she urgently whispered to Gul. "Help me tie up her feet. It's the manager. I saw him come down the corridor."

Tears started streaming down Farah's face, and Gul felt a pang of guilt for her earlier harshness toward the woman. She gently patted her on the shoulder, attempting to console her. "Don't worry—it's just a decoy," she whispered, and they heard the man approaching from outside.

"Quick, help her sit on the floor the way she was before!" Palwasha ordered, turning off the desk lamp just as they had found it upon entering the room. "We don't have time to tie your hands, Farah, so just put them behind your back and pretend!" She quickly hid behind the heavy curtains.

The door opened. The man grumbled to himself, and they could only guess that he was surprised he had forgotten to lock the door behind him. The girls listened carefully in the dark as he paced the room. Gul held her breath, aware he was standing nearby, tightly clasping her hand over her mouth, not even daring to blink.

"Well, well, well, Madam Farah," the man's voice echoed in the room. "For a moment, I thought I wouldn't find you here. But how could you escape when you were all tied up? You didn't know I forgot to lock the room, or else you would have attempted something funny, eh? I suppose you're smarter than your pathetic father." The man's words were filled with menace. Farah remained still on the floor, leaning against the fireplace, her eyes fixed on the manager's every move, silently praying that he wouldn't notice the rope around her ankle had come loose. The man's eyes were fixed on Farah. "Just wanted to let you know that the running of the guesthouse would go on as usual, and don't worry, no one will miss you," he sneered. Farah could only groan in despair. "No use, dear, no one is coming to your rescue. It's a shame you interfered with Baaz's and my plan and tipped that assistant commissioner Najeeb. Not a smart move on your part!" His tone got increasingly threatening.

Gul glanced at Palwasha at the mention of Najeeb and recalled her conversation with him, realizing why he was so adamant they stay away from the guesthouse. Gul peered through the chink in the curtain: It seemed like the man could inflict bodily harm on Farah at any moment. She saw him standing lighting a cigarette, looking around as if he had sensed that there was someone else in the room. Taking a long puff, he stood very still as if trying to listen to something which could not be seen. Gul and Palwasha kept still.

He shrugged and focused his attention back to his captor. "The infallible Farah has become fallible!" he leered. Farah looked at him helplessly. The man took a step closer to her. "Don't you have anything to say, dear Farah? But of course, you can't. How foolish of me," And with one quick motion, he ripped the duct tape off, making Farah wince in pain.

"Let my father go, please! He's old and sick, I beg of you!" The man grew furious and banged his fist on the desk, startling Farah and causing the girls to tremble in fear behind the curtain. For a few seconds, there was silence with no one moving. Surprisingly, Farah then cried out in anger, "I've done everything you asked me to do! I sent the jewels with the girls—put their lives at stake! What more do you want from me?"

The man calmly took out a paper from his pocket. "Well, for starters, I want you to sign these papers. Let's just say it's an extended leave of absence from your side," he said, slapping the paper on top of the desk.

"What's this for?" she asked, her voice filled with trepidation.

The manager snorted in disdain. "This, my dear, is the paper signing away your property in my name. I've had enough of taking orders from you and your father. No more!" His bitterness seeped into his tone, revealing a long-held grudge against Farah. "I dedicated myself to your father's business, giving my all. But when he became incapacitated, instead of appointing me in charge, what did he do? He entrusted all the power to you, a young girl fresh out of college with no experience. And you treated me like dirt! But not anymore! Just sign these papers, and you can be reunited with your father. Otherwise, he's going to suffer just because you didn't do as I told you," the man lashed out. His breathing was heavy, consumed by revenge.

Farah's fear intensified, her eyes pleading with the man. "Please, no. Don't hurt him. He's very sick. I will sign the paper, but only when I see him first," she pleaded desperately.

The man looked at her and let out a sinister laugh. "I must say, you have the guts to make a deal with me. Hmm, all right, since you insist, I will bring your father here. But that will be the last order you have given," he sneered. He picked up the paper, folded it, and put it in his coat pocket before leaving the room.

The key turned in the lock, and the sisters exchanged horrified looks. Now they were trapped inside the room. Gul felt anxiety welling up within her, and cautiously, she stepped out from behind the curtains and surveyed their surroundings. Sure enough, no one else was in the room except for Farah, who remained in the same position.

"You didn't tell us anything about your father. Even now, when you were asking for our help, you weren't being completely honest with us!" Gul accused Farah. "And you, Palwasha, told me to trust her!"

Palwasha's voice trembled, feeling betrayed. "Farah! You knew about this all along? You intentionally used us? Put so many girls' lives at stake to smuggle gems and other illicit items? You're spreading nothing but evil in our valley!"

Farah remained silent with her head down, weeping.

Palwasha's disgust for Farah grew stronger. "Out of all the places, you had to come here and exploit our girls and their innocence for your evil plans!" Palwasha couldn't believe she had been deceived.

"Shhh, Palwasha, stop it. Our priority now is finding a way out of here, not getting into arguments with her." Gul tried to pacify her sister even though she felt the same anger toward the woman.

Before the sisters could take any action, they heard the man's voice outside the door, engaged in conversation with someone. The girls immediately turned their attention to Farah, with Gul motioning toward the door. Farah nodded, confirming that the manager had returned. The sisters hastily positioned themselves behind the curtains again, their hearts pounding in their chests as they remained completely still. The door swung open, and the manager nonchalantly reentered the room as if taking a leisurely stroll. Farah, her vision blurred by tears, glanced past the manager's figure. A chair was being pushed by a skinny, short man. Seated in the wheelchair was an elderly man, his frail body slumped forward. It was evident that he was extremely ill and would require support to sit up straight. However, the skinny man displayed no concern or compassion. Gul could see all the three people through the slight chink between the curtain panels. But Palwasha, who couldn't see anything, squeezed her sister's hand.

The manager turned to Farah. "Well, here is your father. A nice family reunion, I must say," he joked sarcastically. The skinny man after wheeling the chair in, retreated quickly, closing the door behind softly. With one look at her father, Farah knew that something was not right.

Farah cried out in horror, her voice growing increasingly hysterical. "What have you done to my father? Why is he sitting like this? He can't breathe on his own!" Her desperation was evident, but the manager seemed unaffected.

"You want to cry? Then cry! Nobody will hear you, and it won't change a thing," he callously declared, placing the paper back on the desk. "I brought your old man, and now you've seen him."

Farah glared at the manager. "No! I won't sign the paper! First, tell me why he's not conscious!" Her voice quivered with emotion.

In a menacing manner, the manager took a step closer to her but then hesitated. Instead, he turned and removed the oxygen mask from the old man's face, worsening his already dire condition. Gul's horror intensified as she witnessed the distressing scene unfolding before her eyes. Her heart raced uncontrollably as if desperately trying to break free from her chest. Farah screamed in anguish as she saw her father coughing and struggling for breath. His body convulsed as he fought to inhale precious air. In her desperation, Farah attempted to rise but stumbled, her legs entangled in the loose rope. Farah's sudden movement caught the manager off guard, momentarily surprising him.

His anger flared even more, his eyes flashing with fury as he confronted Farah. "Where do you think you're going? Sign the paper now, or your old man will suffer even more," he growled, standing menacingly in front of her with his feet planted firmly apart. Farah winced in pain, her ankle throbbing even more after the fall. However, her priority was to save her father, no matter the cost.

Through her tears, she made a desperate plea. "I will sign the papers, but please, put the oxygen mask on him first!"

The man remained unmoved, showing no concern for the old man's suffering. "Sign the paper first, and then you and your father can be free," he coldly responded.

"Aaaccchooo!"

The sudden sneeze echoed through the room, startling the man like a deer caught in headlights. He stood very still, taken aback; his grip on the papers loosened, causing them to roll onto the carpet, coming to rest near Farah's feet.

CHAPTER 21

The Escape

"What, who?" The man was stunned by the sudden attack.

Before he could react, Gul had lunged at him with all her strength from behind the curtains. Meanwhile, Palwasha also jumped in, taking charge, and unleashed a series of punches to the man's stomach—her fists like those of a skilled boxer preparing for a match. Despite their efforts, the man proved to be a strong opponent. He fought back fiercely, enduring kicks and punches from all directions. In the midst of the struggle, Palwasha cried out in pain. Her cap had fallen off during the scuffle, and the man had seized a tight grip on her hair. With a swift and enraged motion, Palwasha swept her right hand over the desk, grabbing hold of a marble pencil holder. Without hesitation, she swung her hand and struck the man's head. A dull thud resounded as the pencil holder made contact, causing the man to yell in pain and double over, clutching his head with both hands in pain. Seizing the opportunity, Palwasha struck him again, and this time, the man collapsed onto the carpet, lying motionless. There was a moment of tense silence that enveloped the room after the chaotic struggle. Gul gazed at her sister, a mixture of surprise and concern evident on her face. Palwasha, still reeling from the shock of her own actions, knelt down beside the motionless man, her heart pounding with fear and regret.

"Is he? Is he…dead?" Palwasha stammered, her voice quivering. She looked up at her sister, tears welling up in her eyes. "I swear I didn't mean to." Her gaze returned to the man, overwhelmed by a flood of emotions. Although the sight of a man sprawled on the carpet unconscious was not pretty at all, Gul realized the gravity of the situation; with newfound determination, she sprang into action and grabbed the rope.

"Palwasha, he is not dead!" She felt the man's pulse. "Just conked out. Please snap out of it, and help me tie him up!"

Feeling relieved, Palwasha hurriedly got to her feet. Both the girls worked swiftly and efficiently, securing the man's wrists tightly. As they finished tying him up, Palwasha glanced back at Farah, who was still seated on the floor, still sobbing.

"We need to get out of here," Palwasha whispered to Gul, her voice filled with urgency. "We can't stay in this room any longer. We have to find Zarmeena and get her father to safety."

Gul nodded, her focus unwavering. Together, they helped Farah to her feet. "Farah, is there another exit out of the guesthouse? We need to avoid any potential danger and find help as soon as possible."

Farah hesitated for a moment, her brow furrowed in thought. "Yes, there's a back door on the ground floor that leads to a narrow alley behind the guesthouse. It's not frequently used, but it could be our best chance to leave unnoticed. We'll have to be cautious."

Gul, who had been trying to devise a plan for their next steps, looked at Farah with a glare. "Yes, but we are not leaving here without my cousin. She is not with the rest of the girls. She went missing tonight, and we followed her car. It's parked at the back!" Gul's irritation was mounting as they had made no progress in finding their cousin. Time was slipping away, and with dawn approaching, they knew that they had to hurry before the morning and kitchen staff clocked in.

Farah appeared confused. "But why would anyone from the guesthouse want to kidnap your cousin?" She gazed at the sisters, clearly puzzled. Suddenly, the intercom in the room started buzzing, startling everyone.

Gul turned to Farah, annoyed. "Well…? It's your room. Who could be calling at this hour?"

Farah's eyes widened with desperation. "I remember when the manager tied me up, he was talking to someone on the intercom. But I don't know who it was. He seemed unhappy and kept mentioning how careless he had been. He was asking about the whereabouts of the cargo."

"That's all you heard?" Palwasha countered, her tone accusatory as if blaming Farah for not being able to decipher the conversation on the other end of the intercom.

"Okay, Farah, tell me, how many rooms are there in this wing?" Gul asked in a friendlier tone, realizing that offending Farah would not get them anywhere, especially not until they found Zarmeena. "And please, no funny business," she added sweetly as a reminder.

"There are just nine rooms on this floor, and this one is the ninth. The only exit is through the elevator," Farah answered, trying to be as helpful as possible. She knew her father needed medical attention, and the girls were her only hope. Gul smiled, though it wasn't a genuinely friendly smile. It was more to acknowledge that Farah was cooperating.

"Okay, Farah, we are trusting you. We will go and check the rest of the rooms. While we're gone, keep the door locked and don't open it for anyone. And when we come back, we will knock five times in a row. That will be our code," Gul explained. With that, the sisters slipped out of the room and into the hallway.

"I wonder why we didn't just lock the room ourselves," Palwasha whispered as they hurried toward the end of the corridor to check room 301 first.

"We can't leave the two locked up, in case something happens to us," Gul remarked in a nonchalant manner, trying not to dwell on the possibilities herself.

Palwasha blinked, unable to believe what her sister had just said. Upon reaching the end of the corridor, Palwasha tried the knob of the first room on the right, and it opened without a sound. She stood still, trying to listen for any sounds coming from inside, but all was quiet. Holding her breath, she peered in. Although there was no light in the room, the light from the balcony streamed in, and she could see that the room was empty, as if no one had been there for a while. Slowly, she moved out, closing the door behind her and motioning for her sister to check the room on the opposite side. It was the same as the previous one; it was empty. Her heart sinking, she saw her sister, who was already standing in front of the third door. Gul cautiously turned the handle, and the door opened; silently, she stepped inside. As her eyes adjusted to the dimly lit room, her sixth sense told her that the room was occupied. She looked around desperately, searching for a hiding spot, when the door of the dressing room suddenly opened. A girl stepped out, and Gul barely had time to react. The two girls stood there, looking at each other. Gul's throat went dry, but before she could make a move or say anything, the girl chuckled.

"Palwasha, is that you?" the girl asked, not scared but rather surprised. She moved forward, holding a dress in her hand, a cynical smile on her face. "I guess Farah convinced you to go to Dubai after all." Palwasha, who had been standing guard outside, heard her name and instantly recognized the voice. Silently, she stepped inside and walked over to where Gul was standing. The girl holding the dress couldn't understand what was happening for a moment. Her eyes darted back and forth between Gul and Palwasha's faces, a look of utter disbelief on her face. Her mouth opened and closed at a loss for words. When she finally managed to speak, her voice came out as a croak.

"What in the world is happening?" she asked, feeling terrified as if she was suddenly seeing double.

Palwasha stepped forward, standing in front of the girl. "Nothing out of the ordinary, dear," she commented, a hint of sarcasm in her voice. "I am Palwasha, and that's Gul, my twin sister. So don't be scared. I'm a bit confused, though. Weren't you supposed to be at the airport already, flying to Dubai?" Palwasha wondered if Farah had withheld some information or if she was just bluffing. The girl, Hina, was the same person who had mistakenly handed Gul the dress in the factory's parking lot, thinking she was Palwasha. Hina, now composed, looked at the sisters with raised eyebrows.

"Isn't it a bit late for you girls to join us for the exhibition? You weren't present at the fittings, and as far as I remember, Anoosha had the final list of models, and your names weren't on it. But I suppose you've always been Farah's favorite, so she must have added you at the last moment," Hina rambled on, carefully folding her dress and placing it in a trolley bag on the bed.

Gul's voice turned into a fierce whisper as she asked, "What did you just say? Who made the final list?" She pulled her sister back and snatched the dress from Hina's hand. A bit taken aback by Gul's sudden outburst and her intense gaze, Hina glanced at Palwasha, hoping for some clarity on the situation.

"I...I said the girls were—" Hina stammered, stepping back in confusion. She couldn't understand why Gul was behaving this way, but before she could explain further, Gul interrupted her.

"No, stop. Just tell me who you said made the final list." Gul's anger was palpable.

Sitting on the edge of the bed, Hina looked at Palwasha, her own voice trembling. "Anoosha...I said Anoosha. You know her, Palwasha, don't you? She is your friend." Hina sought confirmation from Palwasha, still unaware of why Gul was so worked up.

Gul let out a long sigh and sat next to Hina, shaking her head in disbelief.

Palwasha was stunned at the loss of words.

All this time, Anoosha had been pretending to help. But it was all a carefully crafted lie.

Palwasha felt a deep sense of betrayal.

"Palwasha!" Gul hissed, clicking her fingers in front of Palwasha's face. "Now is not the time to dwell on this, we need to find Zarmeena and get out of here fast." Still shocked by the revelation, without uttering a word, she silently got up like a robot. Gul turned to Hina. "You have to come with us!" She gestured the girl to follow them, but Hina stood her ground, giving them a stubborn look.

"Hey, you guys, this is not your call. If you don't want to go to Dubai, that's your choice. I am the showstopper, and this is going to be a once-in-a-lifetime chance for me. Why should I just throw it away because you are telling me to!" With that, she plopped herself in the middle of the bed, and with a smug expression, she began folding the dress on the bed, oblivious to the tension in the room.

Gul's patience was wearing thin, with a stern expression, she grabbed Hina by the shoulders and shook. "Listen, if you don't do as we say, you and the girls will become mere pawns in a money laundering scheme. We have to leave this place right now!" Gul felt like slapping the girl at that point.

Wriggling her shoulder free, the girl stood up, almost whining. "But my seat was booked, and the manager was supposed to take me to the airport!" She held the dress against her as if it were her lifeline. Losing patience, Gul motioned Palwasha to talk some sense into the girl.

Palwasha, who was standing quietly in the background, let out a sigh. "Hina, look you don't understand the gravity of the situation. You going to a fashion show is just a facade—please trust us on this. The manager will soon be in police custody, so please trust us!"

"But—" Hina attempted to protest, but Gul pushed her out the room before she could say more.

"No ifs and buts, Hina, and for God's sake, please keep quiet and stay close to us," Gul instructed.

The three girls then slipped out of the room in a single file, with Gul leading the way, Palwasha at the end, and Hina sandwiched between them. The corridor remained eerily quiet, but Gul knew it wouldn't be long before someone noticed that the manager and Farah's father were missing from their designated locations. Sensing the urgency, Gul quickly checked the rest of the rooms with Hina and Palwasha following closely behind. However, all they found were empty rooms.

Gul's heart sank at the realization that the men must have a hiding place where they were keeping Zarmeena. "Oh God, let her be safe," she prayed silently.

Confused, Hina whispered to Palwasha, "What is she doing? I told you all the girls have left. It's only me now, and I was supposed to leave by midmorning. Gul won't find the girls here!"

"We're looking for our cousin," Palwasha replied curtly without divulging any more information. After all that had transpired, she was still unsure whom to trust. Back in the room, the girls quickly assessed the manager's condition.

"He regained a bit of consciousness but then passed out again," Farah informed, her worry evident. "But I'm worried about my father. His condition is worsening." Fear for her father consumed Farah, and she felt the pain in her ankle intensify. The old man certainly looked pale. Palwasha hurriedly checked the man's pulse, her heart sinking as she felt its weakness. To her horror, she noticed that the oxygen level was dangerously low with the needle on the gauge nearly reaching the red mark. Despite the looming uncertainty surrounding Zarmeena's whereabouts, the sisters had made up their minds. The deteriorating condition of Farah's father took precedence.

"Palwasha, listen. It's almost dawn, and it's not safe to stay here any longer. We need to leave. Farah's father does not look good at all—we need to get him out now," Gul said. Now she turned to Farah. "Please do as you're told and don't make any fuss." She looked pointedly at Hina. With that she walked to where the manger was lying, pushing him on his side with all her might.

Puzzled, Palwasha leaned forward. "Gul, what do you have in mind? Why are we rolling him up like a kebab?"

Gul shot her an angry glance. "We're not leaving him here. And instead of making jokes, ask Hina to help us. We can use the curtains as a makeshift hammock to carry him."

CHAPTER 22

The Strange Group

The journey was nerve-racking as they struggled with the manager's dead weight. The two girls took turns, almost dragging their burden across the corridor and into the elevator. Hina pushed the wheelchair, accompanied by Farah who hobbled along, doing her best to keep up. The elevator was spacious enough to accommodate the strange little group, although they had to position the manager in a sitting position leaning against the elevator wall. Palwasha stood next to him, ensuring that he didn't slump to one side.

"Why does he have to fall on my side?" she muttered with disgust, nudging the man back into position with her knee.

Once they reached the ground level, Palwasha took it upon herself to assess the situation in the hallway. Before anyone could object, she swiftly moved to the front and peered out of the elevator. With dawn approaching, she anticipated that some of the guesthouse staff, especially the chefs and their helpers, might already be awake. Palwasha motioned for the group to remain still. Tiptoeing out and reaching the atrium, she leaned against a pillar as she scanned the corridor, ensuring it was clear. Though they could hear the faint sound of muted conversation coming from down the hallway, there was no one present at that moment.

It must be coming from the kitchen. The morning staff are already here. I need to hurry before someone comes out.

She quickly retraced her steps back to the elevator where the rest of the group was anxiously waiting, huddled together. As Palwasha looked at the unusual group in the confined space of the elevator, a sudden wave of amusement washed over her. Despite trying to stifle it, she burst into a fit of silent laughter.

A suave woman with a sprained ankle, a father breathing through an oxygen mask, a girl aspiring to be a showstopper, and last but not least, that buffoon of a man wrapped up in a curtain.

Taken aback by Palwasha's sudden fit, Farah and Hina looked at her with their mouths open. Palwasha, embarrassed, struggled to regain her composure as she placed her hand over her mouth. "Bad timing," she rattled sheepishly.

Avoiding eye contact, Palwasha joined her sister and helped push the unconscious manager out into the hallway. "I know it's a serious situation, but sometimes when I'm nervous, I tend to laugh uncontrollably. I didn't mean to make light of the situation." Her voice was apologetic.

As they dragged the manager along the hallway floor, Gul, who was having difficulty holding onto the curtain due to the unsupported weight of the unconscious manager. "Shh, Palwasha, stop being childish and hold onto the curtain tight please," Gul urged, still struggling to maintain her balance and handle the weight of the man. Both she and her sister stumbled out into the open through the back door. It was already dawn, and it felt as if they had spent a lifetime inside the building.

Palwasha opened the trunk, and with the help of Hina, they hauled the man up into it.

"That was close," Gul remarked, banging the trunk shut as the man started groaning. "He is waking up. Thank God he's alive."

Palwasha shook her head and muttered, "Yeah, or else I would have gone to jail," shuddering at the thought.

Meanwhile, Gul rechecked the gauge on the oxygen tank of the old man. Concerned about the man's worsening condition, she got Hina to help her. "Hina, help me with him." And together, the girls were able to make Farah's father as comfortable as possible in the back seat alongside Farah.

Once behind the steering wheel, Gul noticed that Palwasha was still standing outside.

"Now what?" she muttered. Getting out of the car, she went up to her sister. "Palwasha, we need to leave right now!" But Palwasha was pointing toward Zarmeena's car, staring.

Gul followed Palwasha's gaze and felt a rush of adrenaline rush through her body. Sure enough, a piece of dark-blue cloth was sticking out from underneath the tarp.

"Zarmeena was wearing blue today… I mean, yesterday!" Palwasha rushed toward the car with Gul following closely at her heels. With trembling fingers, the girls hurriedly untied the tarp, pushing it away to expose the side of the car. And there, in a fetal position, gagged and bound, was Zarmeena.

"Zarmeena!" Palwasha shouted, desperately trying to open the door, but it wouldn't budge. She banged on the window, hoping to draw Zarmeena's attention.

Gul was horrified at the sight as she realized that despite Palwasha banging and shouting, Zarmeena didn't move; lying very still. Frantically, Palwasha tried all four doors, but they were locked. She banged on the window again, not caring if someone heard the commotion inside, but it seemed that Zarmeena was completely unaware of her surroundings. Gul looked around frantically and spotted a small iron rod near a small boulder. Grabbing the bar, she ran around the car and smashed the rod against the driver's side window. The first hit created a large weblike crack, which she followed with another blow to shatter the weakened glass. Gul carefully reached her hand through the broken window, being cautious of the sharp edges, and unlocked the car.

Gul climbed into the car and removed the gag from Zarmeena's mouth, untying her cousin's hands and feet, checking to ensure she was breathing. She let out a sigh of relief, almost near to tears. "Palwasha, help me get her out. She won't wake up; I think she was drugged or something." With some effort, they managed to extricate Zarmeena from her car and place her in their own vehicle.

Meanwhile, Farah's impatience grew. "You girls need to hurry. We can't afford to waste any more time," she exclaimed, tapping the gauge that indicated the oxygen tank was empty.

"Hold your horses, Farah!" Gul sharply turned to Farah, her face flushed with anxiety. "If something happens to our cousin, it's going to be all your fault!"

The sisters had placed their cousin in the front seat, with Palwasha quickly finding a half-used water bottle and splashing some water on Zarmeena's face. The sudden cold shock caused Zarmeena to groan, and Palwasha began rubbing her cousin's hands and feet. Remembering the manager's conversation about the "package" in the trunk during the intercom call, Gul's mind raced. Instead of moving forward, she hit the brakes again and swiftly got out of the car, running back toward Zarmeena's car. Quickly she opened the trunk, but the trunk was empty. Gul scowled, contemplating the situation. But just as she was about to close the trunk, she noticed that the lining at the base was slightly askew as if hastily arranged. She pulled up the lining, revealing a hidden compartment in the middle. Nestled within that compartment were traditional embroidered slippers. For a moment, Gul's head reeled with surprise, and in frustration, she picked up one slipper and threw it on the ground with force. Never in their lives had the girls seen such glittering red beauties lying scattered on the ground in front of them.

"Oh my," Hina uttered in amazement. Gul herself was taken aback, as if she had produced those beautiful gems from a pile of slippers through some magic trick. Palwasha, realizing that it would take time for Gul alone to pick up the gems, scrambled out of the car, and joined Gul in gathering the rubies, stuffing them into her pockets.

"Oh my god!" Palwasha panted, picking up the last of the scattered ruby glinting in the early morning sunlight.

With the rubies secured, the girls were finally on their way.

Zarmeena, who was sandwiched between her two cousins, moaned loudly as she regained more consciousness. "Ugh, where am I? And my head!" she groaned again, holding her head. Zarmeena looked pale and blinked rapidly as the bright sunlight was too much for her eyes to handle.

Palwasha gently pushed her cousin toward herself. "It's okay, Zarmeena. I don't know, but you might have a concussion, so just relax and keep still. You will be okay," Palwasha consoled her cousin.

"Concussion?" Zarmeena was puzzled and tried to sit up straight, but a bout of dizziness hit her, making her cry out. "Oh, Palwasha, this hurts," she moaned, feeling groggy and instantly closed her eyes, leaning against her cousin's shoulder.

Palwasha looked over her cousin at her sister, and it was clear that she was worried about Zarmeena and Farah's father. In reply, Gul hit the gas pedal hard, exceeding the speed limit. This time, Gul had taken the main Mall road toward the city center.

Hina, who was sitting quietly sulking in the back, cleared her throat. "Umm…would it be asking too much if you can drop me off at the next bus stop? I can easily get a ride to my house from there," she added.

Appalled, Palwasha turned in her seat, scowling at the girl. "Are you for real?" Her voice was full of distaste.

But Hina was unfazed. "I have done nothing wrong here, I presume. So why drag me into it?" she retorted stubbornly. Palwasha rolled her eyes knowing fully well that it was no use trying to make the girl think unselfishly.

Gul was quiet, concentrating on the driving, and made it to the city hospital in record time. As soon as she stopped the car in front of the emergency ward, they were surrounded by paramedical staff, and within minutes, Zarmeena, Farah, and her father were wheeled inside.

CHAPTER 23

The Man in the Hospital

Palwasha, who had finished giving details to the paramedical staff, saw Hina slinking out of the car. She quickly thanked the staff and made her way around the car, blocking Hina's path.

"Not so fast, my dear. Where do you think you're going?" Palwasha stood facing Hina, her expression defiant.

Hina looked embarrassed and gave a sheepish smile to Palwasha. "My parents will be worried about me." She tried to come up with an excuse.

But Palwasha wasn't going to fall for it. She took Hina's hand and pushed her back toward the car. "Don't worry, showstopper. Your parents will be informed that you're safe and sound with us. And please, would you mind emptying your pockets?" Palwasha demanded, extending her arms towards Hina with a knowing expression on her face. For a second, Hina just stood there, seemingly weighing her options. Then all of a sudden, she made a dash toward the hospital exit gate. But Palwasha was quick on her feet and instantly pursued Hina. However, Hina bumped headlong into a figure who had just gotten out of his jeep and was heading toward the emergency ward.

Palwasha instantly recognized the person and, with all her might, shouted at the man, "Ali, Ali, stop that girl!" Ali, who had seen Palwasha from a distance, without missing a beat, had an iron grip on Hina's arm. Hina struggled like a wildcat, but it was futile fighting against Ali, who was a bit surprised and, at the same time, relieved after seeing Palwasha. Hina had stopped her fiery protest and was now standing quietly scowling at Palwasha.

"Oh, thank God I saw you, Ali. Otherwise, I would have had to—" Ali held up his hand, signaling her to keep quiet, and immediately dialed Najeeb's number while still holding onto Hina.

"Hello, Najeeb…yeah, leave everything and come to the city hospital ASAP." He spoke into the phone. He looked at Palwasha with concern, "Where is Gul?" He put his hand over the speaker of the phone, awaiting Palwasha's response, dreading any bad news.

Palwasha knew that Najeeb must have asked about Gul too, as Ali had informed him of her presence. With a knowing smile at Ali, instead of answering directly, she leaned over and removed Ali's hand from the speaker. She shouted loudly enough for Najeeb to hear her clearly on the other end of the line, "Gul is fine! She's inside the building, and no, she is not hurt! And Zarmeena is fine too!" With that, she moved back, a hint of a smile lurking at the corner of her mouth. The conversation was one-way and very short, knowing well that Najeeb had been worried about them, especially Gul. Satisfied, she turned her attention toward Hina, and before she could utter a word, Ali interjected with a volley of questions, which took her by surprise.

Still holding on to Hina, Ali said, "Where have you girls been? Who is this girl? Why is Gul inside? What are you doing at the hospital?"

Despite understanding Ali's frustration, Palwasha couldn't help but meet his gaze defiantly. "Our phones were dead and—" Suddenly, she reached forward and pulled Hina closer, digging her hands into Hina's shirt pocket. Palwasha retrieved the stones and held them up to Ali. "And we found these," she declared, her obstinacy shining through as if the discovery of the rubies was the reason their phones had died. Ali was momentarily taken aback, but he quickly tightened his grip on Hina and shot Palwasha a warning look.

"Put that away! This is a public place!" he ordered. Simultaneously, he signaled to his sepoy to call a lady police constable, suspecting that the girls had stumbled upon something significant. By the time the lady constable arrived to escort Hina to the police station, the girl was almost in tears. Palwasha couldn't help but feel sorry for her. She knew it wasn't fair to Hina, and she wanted to explain everything to Ali. However, before she could say anything, Gul emerged from the building with a concerned expression on her face.

"Gul! Gul! Ali is here!" She waved to her sister.

Gul, looking tense, spotted them and waved, relieved to see a familiar face of authority. "Thank God! Ali, you are here. We need your help."

Ali looked at Gul's disheveled appearance and suddenly realized that both girls were wearing some kind of uniform. But before anyone could engage in conversation, they heard a muffled sound coming from the trunk of the car. Everyone stood still, and then it happened again, even louder this time. Ali looked at the car and then at the girls, taken aback. Gul and Palwasha exchanged horrified looks.

"Oh gosh, we totally forgot about the manager!" Gul cried out moving swiftly toward the car. She yanked the trunk open, and there he was, the manager, all tied up, his face red with frustration and anger.

The moment he saw the girls, he lashed out at them, "How dare you tie me up like that? You will pay for it!" The manager seethed in anger, astounded that a couple of girls could take him prisoner and disrupt his meticulously planned scheme. "Let me out!" he shouted again, attempting to free his hands, unaware of the man standing beside the two girls. "Let me out, you stupid girls!" And then he noticed Ali, standing there with his hands at his sides, staring at him sternly.

For a moment, the man was at a loss for words, but then he started struggling once more. "And who are you? Their accomplice?" he shouted in frustration. Ali, not in his uniform but always armed, took out his gun and released the safety catch, pointing it at the man. Seeing the gun, the man abruptly stopped shouting, his eyes darting back and forth, finally resting on Ali's face. "Who are you? I will call the police! You people have kidnapped me!"

Ali, with a piercing look, holstered his gun. "Don't worry, buddy. You're in safe hands now. I am the police." The manager stared dumbfounded at Ali, recognition slowly dawning on him. He couldn't place Ali at first but soon realized he was Police Officer Ali Faraz. The color drained from the manager's face, and all he could do was mutter nonsensical words. He knew he wouldn't be able to escape this time.

An hour had passed since Ali's call to Najeeb, and by now, Ali had taken the girls to the waiting lounge of the private wing, where Zarmeena was admitted for observation for the next twenty-four hours. The girls sat down in the lounge as Najeeb entered, his exhausted appearance evident from his bloodshot eyes and ragged expression. It was clear that he hadn't slept a wink and had been through a lot. Gul, who was on the phone talking to her father, noticed Najeeb's arrival accompanied by two police constables. Despite his concern for his friends, Najeeb maintained a composed demeanor, not displaying too much emotion, Najeeb gestured for the girls to take their seats, and one of the constables began asking questions while taking notes. Ali had also joined the group after ensuring security at Farah's and her father's room and that the manager was moved to a secure area after a preliminary medical examination. The girls recounted everything that had transpired since they discovered Zarmeena was missing with Najeeb and Ali interjecting at intervals. They shared the details of finding Hina and what she and Farah had disclosed about the girls' plans to travel to Dubai that evening. Ali immediately contacted his counterpart in Islamabad to provide information about Anoosha and the girls staying at the airport hotel, including their flight details.

Palwasha couldn't help but feel guilty and regretful for falling into Anoosha's trap. Tears welled up in her eyes as she looked at her sister and cousin, expressing her sincere apologies. "I'm truly sorry for all of this. I had no idea that Anoosha was involved in such schemes, luring college girls into exhibitions and modeling shows to launder money and engage in other illicit activities." Her head was in her hands, overwhelmed with guilt and shame.

"Aw come on Palwasha! How could you have known about this? She fooled all of us!" Gul hugged her sister.

Najeeb had remained silent, unsure of what to say to Palwasha. He was torn between consoling her and scolding the sisters for taking such a risk. Gul and Najeeb turned to Ali, who had secretly admired the bravery of the two sisters as they explained their drive to the guesthouse and how they had overpowered the manager, especially highlighting the moment when Palwasha had struck him on the head. Ali cleared his throat as if preparing to deliver a speech.

"You know, Palwasha, you could join the police force through a short commission. The application deadline is at the end of next month!"

The group looked at Ali in bewilderment.

Ali quickly got up, muttering something about Khalil and the doctor. As he walked out the door, he turned back and surprisingly called out to Palwasha, "Do think it over!" before disappearing.

Palwasha, lost in thought of Anoosha's betrayal, had not heard what Ali had said. Looking up at Ali's retreating figure, she wondered aloud, "Think about what?"

But Ali had already left. She let out a soft chuckle and turned to Najeeb. "Is your friend okay? He seemed a bit upset with me. And what is there for me to think over? I know I made a huge mistake by befriending Anoosha, but she helped me a lot with my workshop. It would have been very difficult to arrange funds in such a short span of time without her." Palwasha was upset with herself and at the entire situation, realizing they might not be able to participate in the closing ceremony of the tournament. Gul slid closer to her sister on the sofa and wrapped her arms around her, offering silent comfort. Their silence broke when Ali entered the room, his face flushed with excitement.

"Najeeb, finally good news!" Ali exclaimed, shaking hands with Najeeb eagerly. "We got him!" Najeeb pulled him in for a bear hug, his excitement matching Ali's.

"Where did they find him? Was he still in the building?" Najeeb asked, rising from his chair. "And what about that black onyx Buddha statue?"

Ali's smile faltered slightly, his expression turning dejected. "I'm sorry, buddy. The man was heavily sedated, and the search yielded nothing. They are taking him to the police hospital as there are no beds available here. But we will conduct a thorough search of the building. We may get lucky, and once Baaz regains consciousness, we will find out where he hid the statue."

Both Ali and Najeeb busied themselves with making phone calls, coordinating further actions to search the guesthouse building. Meanwhile, feeling somewhat inadequate in the moment, the sisters excused themselves to visit Zarmeena in the ward. Zarmeena was peacefully sleeping, unaware of the turmoil surrounding them.

Gul looked at her cousin fondly and couldn't help but shudder as the memory of Zarmeena being bound and gagged resurfaced. Palwasha tapped Gul on the shoulder, her voice filled with worry. "Gul, we still have no news about Anoosha and the other girls. I hope the police are able to find them. I really feel for their parents, and I am concerned about Baba's reaction." Palwasha's anxiety was growing, and Gul knew Palwasha was blaming herself for what had happened.

"Palwasha, could you do me a favor? Try to relax and stay here. I need to go and check on Zarmeena's condition with her doctor. If he confirms that she is fine, we will take her home. But for her sake, we need to make her feel comfortable and safe. Your crying won't help her at all. Please gather yourself, and I will be right back." Palwasha nodded, trying to control her tears.

Back in the waiting lounge, which now resembled a mini operation room rather than a visitor's area, a radio transmitter had been set up, and Najeeb had his laptop with him. Six plainclothes men were present, and one of them initially tried to stop Gul from entering. However, Ali gestured for the man to let Gul through. Overwhelmed by the situation, Gul approached Najeeb, who was engrossed in conversation with the men investigating the guesthouse. Concerned about Gul's demeanor, he ended the call, hoping Zarmeena was all right.

"Do you have any news about the girls and Anoosha?" Gul asked, coming straight to the point. "We are worried about them." She nervously glanced around at the bustling activity in the room.

"Yes and no," Najeeb replied cautiously, not wanting to raise false hope. Najeeb realized the gravity of the situation and the impact it had on Gul and felt a pang of guilt for not being available when she needed him the most.

"Gul, I'm sorry if my absence caused you distress. I understand how you must have felt trying to reach me and not getting any response. I assure you that I wasn't intentionally withholding information. It's just that the situation was complicated, and I needed to gather accurate details before sharing anything," Najeeb explained, his voice filled with sincerity.

Gul took a moment to collect herself, wiping away her tears. "I know you have your reasons, Najeeb. It's just that everything felt so chaotic, and I was worried sick about Zarmeena and the other girls. I couldn't bear the thought of something happening to them while we were unable to reach you."

I am sorry again for not being there when you needed me. Honestly, when I saw the missed calls and realized you, Palwasha, and Zarmeena were not at home, you cannot imagine the panic I felt. I was in Landikotal—you know how the network can be unreliable there. And the worst part was that when I tried to call you or Palwasha, nobody picked up the phone. I can't describe the thoughts that ran through my mind. I thought something was terribly wrong. I searched for you like a madman," Najeeb explained in anguish.

Gul managed a smile through her tears, which threatened to fall again. "I apologize for venting my anger on you. I was worried too," she admitted.

Najeeb held Gul's gaze, offering her a lopsided smile. "I can see that now. Today taught me not to take anything for granted. Gul, I don't want to take our feelings for granted."

Gul blushed slightly, maintaining eye contact. She held his hand. "Neither do I, Najeeb."

CHAPTER 24

The Black Statue

That evening, things started moving quickly: Anoosha was apprehended at the airport by the authorities, later confessing to working for the manager of the guesthouse, who was working closely with Baaz. It was revealed that the girls they hired for modeling were being used to launder money and smuggle precious stones out of the country. Gul and Palwasha sat in their living room, accompanied by Zarmeena, relieved that their cousin was back home and feeling well. Najeeb and Ali had gone out to get some food as no one was in the mood to cook. Zarmeena, reclining on the easy chair, flipped through TV channels.

"You know, girls, I feel jealous that you two had all the fun and adventure while I was conked out in the back seat of my car. I should have been with you, hunting down that Baaz character," Zarmeena remarked, making a face. "It's really not fair. Next time, mind you, I'm going with you girls." She winked at her cousins.

Palwasha playfully threw a peanut shell at her cousin, narrowly missing her. "Listen, cousin, you weren't conked out—you were just getting your beauty sleep. In fact, my dear cousin, if you had not eaten so much and gone outside to walk off that food, we might not have been able to catch Baaz at all!"

"Gosh, yes, it was scary." Zarmeena sat up straight. "Did I tell you guys exactly what happened? Did I? Did I?" Zarmeena insisted.

Before the girls could stop Zarmeena from narrating the adventure again for the umpteenth time, she perched the bowl of crackers on her knees, sitting comfortably in the easy chair, enjoying the attention.

"I was walking up the trail to the barn when I saw a flickering light in the barn," Zarmeena paused, trying to put a dramatic feel to her storytelling.

Palwasha winked at her sister. "And then what happened, Zarmeena?"

"So I thought I should investigate, and as I went in, I thought I heard somebody inside. Before I could say or do anything, that Baaz man suddenly had my hand in a tight grip and was holding a gun against me!"

"You must have been scared, Zarmeena!" Gul interjected, looking at her cousin with relief.

"Well, yes, of course. And then he made me walk all the way down the trail, although he was limping, and he had a bad gash on his face too. But I'm not sure what he was doing in our barn. I think he was hiding from the police," Zarmeena thought aloud, "but anyways, he saw the cars and made me get the car keys. In fact, when we reached the driveway, we heard the two of you calling out my name. That's when he made me go around the house. While you girls were out at the back near the base of the trail, he took me inside to get the car keys, and then we backtracked our way to where the cars were parked."

"And all this time, you and Baaz could see us looking for you." Palwasah felt like an idiot at that thought.

"Yeah, he was holding a gun on me, so I couldn't do anything. And when you girls went inside to look for me, we got in my car and took off!"

"Phew, Zarmeena, that would have felt awful. We also found your phone and thought you might have gone down the trail and hurt yourself." Palwasha got up and hugged her cousin. "We are glad that you are back home and safe with us!" Palwasha laughed. "I must say you look better now!"

Zarmeena beamed across the room, looking at her cousins affectionately. "Thank you both for coming after me—otherwise, I might have become part of the smuggled goods traveling across the Arabian Sea." She chuckled.

Gul didn't react. Instead, she raised her hand, motioning for the others to keep quiet as she turned up the volume of the TV. "Girls, look, there's some news about the arrest!"

Zarmeena suddenly raised her hand, motioning toward the TV. "That's Anoosha's photo on the screen. Thank God they arrested her, and now the girls are back safe and sound in their homes," Zarmeena exclaimed, glancing at Palwasha. "I knew you were very concerned about them, but everything turned out fine. However, there's no news of Baaz. It's strange that there's no update on him even though he's in police custody!" Zarmeena sighed, checking her watch and rolling her eyes. "I must say, the boys are slow. We should have gone and gotten the food ourselves. They have a habit of turning up a wee bit late when they are needed."

"They surely are taking their time," Gul replied, flipping through a magazine. As she did, a photo fell from its pages. She picked it up and realized it was the same one Najeeb had selected from the carton. However, her attention quickly shifted back to Zarmeena's ongoing conversation.

"And you know, at first, I thought Baaz was just a homeless person using the barn as a place to crash. But when he pulled out his gun, I realized it was serious business." Zarmeena chatted away, jumping from one subject to another.

"Yes, come to think of it, the barn door is always locked—he must have picked the lock. But why would he specifically choose to hide in a private barn and why not go straight to the guesthouse?" Palwasha pondered aloud.

"Hmmm, I think he was using the barn as a rest stop before going to the guesthouse. He looked tired and injured," Zarmeena added, looking thoughtfully at Palwasha, "but in a way, it was a fortunate coincidence that it was our barn and we caught him at last!" With a satisfied sigh, she turned in her chair and called out to her sister, "Gul, could you please hand me the throw…? Gul!"

But Gul didn't respond. Instead, she abruptly got up, her eyes gleaming with excitement. She glanced at the girls and exclaimed, "You know what? There was a reason Baaz was hiding there!" Without wasting any time, she put on her shoes and cardigan.

Palwasha sat up straight, eyeing her sister. "Gul, tell us what it is. I don't like that look on your face! Gul! I'm talking to you!" However, her sister had already darted out the back door, running as if her life depended on it, disregarding Palwasha's calls.

Zarmeena stood up from her recliner, "Palwasha, what's going on? Is there another kidnapping in progress? I swear I'll leave town if this continues!" Zarmeena rambled. Both she and Palwasha followed the direction of Gul's cell phone's dim light in the distance.

"She's going to the barn," Palwasha exclaimed. She turned to her cousin. "Do you think you can walk to the barn? I don't want to leave you alone, and I don't want Gul to go there all by herself after everything that has happened."

As she contemplated what to do, she was suddenly blinded by the strong beam of a car's headlights. Instantly, she shielded her eyes, trying to see who it was. She heard the car's doors open and shut, but the headlights remained on, causing her pulse to race. She tightened her grip on Zarmeena's hand, both of them struggling to see through the intense light.

"Palwasha! Zarmeena! What's wrong? Why are you girls standing here like this?" Someone shouted their names in concern.

"Oh, thank God, Najeeb! But please, somebody switch off those lights, or I'll go blind!" Palwasha exclaimed, still trying to regain her focus.

"Palwasha! Where is Gul?" Najeeb scanned the area, unable to locate Gul. He looked at Ali, who had been standing near the car, and Ali pointed his cell phone flashlight toward the pathway leading to the barn.

"Hey, Najeeb, I think there's someone up there! Is it Gul?" Ali looked at Palwasha for confirmation, and she nodded silently, unable to find the right words. Najeeb turned and made his way up the slope.

He called out to his friend and cousins, "Ali, go indoors and take the girls with you. I'll be right back with Gul." He saw Ali hesitate for a moment, but he motioned for them to go back inside. "It's okay—lay out the food. We'll be right back." With that, he jogged the rest of the way to the barn. As he climbed the steps, he could hear Gul inside and wondered what she was doing all alone.

"Gul! What are you doing here by yourself?" He burst in, causing Gul to jump back in fear.

"Oh my gosh, Najeeb, don't ever do that to me again. My heart nearly stopped!" she exclaimed, annoyed.

Najeeb looked around, confused by the mess. The large rectangular box was wide open, and the telescope was lying on the floor. Gul stood next to the box, visibly frustrated.

"Okay, what's going on here? You should have been at the house resting!" Najeeb's patience was wearing thin. He had been through a lot in the past two days, trying not to dwell on the worst-case scenario. He was now angry and ready to drag Gul out of the barn. However, to his surprise, she stood there as if she hadn't heard a single word he had just said. Instead, she stared into the distance, fixated on a point in the far corner. Gul jumped over the telescope and got down on her hands and knees, feeling the floor. She had noticed that some of the planks were loose. She attempted to pry them open, but they were difficult to budge.

"Najeeb! Would you mind helping me here?" she shouted, glaring at Najeeb.

Najeeb complied; he knew when Gul was in that mood, she wouldn't listen to anything he had to say. He took out his pocketknife and slid it along the space between the planks. After some tugging and pulling, the crookedly placed plank came loose, causing the other planks to get stuck and giving the impression of an uneven floor. Using the flashlight on his mobile, Najeeb peered into the hollow space. At first, he couldn't see what was inside.

"Look, Najeeb, there's something lying at the bottom," Gul whispered with excitement, hoping her hunch was right.

Najeeb looked at Gul and carefully retrieved the package from inside the hollow space. It was a small black box. Setting down his cell phone, he placed the box on the floor and opened it with caution. Stunned, Najeeb and Gul remained quiet.

Finally, Najeeb broke the silence. "How did you guess it could be here?" he asked, still unsure whether he was dreaming or if it was real. Gul shook her head, still not believing her hunch was right on target. She chuckled, getting up and brushing the dirt off her dress.

"Let's just take it home first, and then we can talk about my hunch over dinner," she smiled, waiting for Najeeb to join her. The rest of the group was waiting in the lounge, wondering what had happened to Najeeb and Gul.

Ali, who was pacing the room, looked at Palwasha. "Exactly why did your sister run to the barn?" Before Palwasha could answer, they heard the two of them come in. Najeeb was holding a box in his hand, looking thoughtful, and Gul trailed behind him with a look of satisfaction on her face.

"I was about to come after you two. What took you so long?" Ali pounced on his friend. "And what is that?" He pointed at the box, looking even more confused.

Najeeb went straight to the table and carefully placed the box in the middle as if he was about to perform a magic trick. "I think it would be only fair if Gul opened the box."

Ali's phone interrupted with a ring.

"Najeeb, sorry for cutting you off like that, but could you wait a minute? I really need to take this call. It's important!" With that request, Ali went out of the room, leaving the four of them looking at the box with curiosity and anticipation.

"Well, what are we supposed to do in the meantime?" Zarmeena commented. She had been feeling much better; in fact, she knew she was the center of attention as everybody was fussing over her after her ordeal. Palwasha, who was feeling hungry now, got up and smiled at her cousin. She knew very well that Zarmeena was loving being pampered.

"Would you like some food, Your Highness? You should eat—otherwise, you might feel lightheaded," she said, bowing in front of her cousin. And the rest of them joined in the light banter.

Gul, who was nearest to the door, suddenly looked up and saw Ali, who was standing in the doorway, observing the happy group.

"Hey, Ali. Come get some food," Gul invited but immediately noticed Ali's facial expression. Ali looked a bit tense. He shifted his weight, first looking at the floor then at his friends, trying to find the right words to break the news.

"Would it be possible for all of you to go to the hospital right now and bring whatever you have in that box if you think it's that important?" he said in a low, clear voice.

"*The hospital?*" everybody cried out all at once.

Najeeb sensed that something important had come up. He turned to the girls. "I think we should go." The tone of his voice made the girls not ask any more questions.

Once they arrived at the hospital, Ali called his secretary, who was waiting for them in the lobby of the private ward. As they entered, the secretary stood up and saluted Ali and Najeeb before handing an envelope to Ali. After bidding them good night, he left the building. The girls grew increasingly worried, unsure of what was happening.

Instead of opening the envelope himself, Ali handed it to Najeeb. "Najeeb, it's yours. You have the right to look at it first."

Najeeb took the envelope, feeling a tremor inside him. He opened it and pulled out a typed paper, reading it carefully. His face turned pale as he absorbed the information, but he remained composed. Gul stepped forward and snatched the paper from Najeeb's trembling hands. Her heart pounded as she scanned the contents, a look of disbelief on her face.

Turning to Najeeb, she exclaimed, "Is this true? How is this possible?" Gul was shocked beyond words, unable to comprehend the report. She waved the paper in front of Ali, demanding answers. "Ali! How can you be so certain? It has only been two days, and you've already confirmed this information?" Gul was unwilling to accept the report without further explanation. Ali looked at his friend, unsure of what to say in response to Gul's disbelief. Without uttering a word, Najeeb moved past them and walked toward the corridor leading to the private ward rooms.

Palwasha and Zarmeena, silent and confused spectators, followed Najeeb down the corridor, unsure of what to expect. Ali motioned for Gul to do the same and then followed the others into the private ward wing. The man sleeping in front of them bore little resemblance to the uncle they once knew except for the familiar scar on his left cheek that had always given him a rakish aura. However, the toll of loss and pain had transformed his face, etching it with permanent marks of grief and suffering.

The four of them stood there, speechless. The man in front of them was the uncle they hadn't heard from in over ten years: Uncle Zargul.

Breaking the silence, Ali spoke in a matter-of-fact tone and gently pressed the man's shoulder, being careful not to cause him any pain. "Khalil, wake up," he said. The man groaned, slowly opening his eyes and attempting to clear his vision. All he saw were five unfamiliar yet beautiful faces. Despite his anxiety, he felt a sense of trust toward these people even though he couldn't recognize them. All he could remember was the news given by the doctor that the boy had died. The surge of grief washed over him, making the tears roll down his weather-beaten face uncontrollably.

"Rehmat…Rehmat is dead," he uttered, his voice filled with sorrow. "My son wanted to come and see the polo match, but I couldn't fulfill his wish." Tears streamed down his face as he closed his eyes, moaning, trying to shut out the pain that consumed him. Those were his final words before slipping into a coma, no longer aware of the world around him.

CHAPTER 25

The Reunion

A week had passed, and life in the valley was slowly returning to normal for the cousins. The discovery of the black onyx statue of Buddha by Gul and Najeeb was being hailed as astounding. The statue, which belonged to the Afghan government, was handed over to the Afghan ambassador during the closing ceremony of the polo tournament, making national and international headlines. Amid the festivities, Palwasha, along with her sister and cousin, showcased their ethnic wear, which was well received by both locals and tourists. An article in the national newspaper even featured them on the front page, praising them as "the gems of the valley."

Zarmeena put down the newspaper and let out a long sigh as she stared out at the valley below. Gul, who was in the midst of packing her bag for an upcoming training academy, grew curious about her cousin's apparent distress. However, Zarmeena remained lost in her thoughts, sighing once again, this time more audibly.

Gul set her shirt down and approached her cousin, expressing her frustration. "Zarmeena, could you please share what's troubling you? You've been sighing and not saying anything!"

But Zarmeena simply smiled, tilting her head to one side as she looked at her cousin with one eye closed. She let out another long sigh and said, "You will be missed, dear cousin. And when you come back, we will embark on another adventure! I'll miss the thrill and excitement!"

Gul smiled and hugged her cousin. "Yes, definitely, but no adventures till I am back!"

ABOUT THE AUTHOR

Raana Sami is a doctor by degree with a military background. Born and bred in the picturesque northern parts of Pakistan, her formative years as a military brat instilled in her a love for adventure and an appreciation for diverse landscapes.

As someone who loves working with kids, Dr. Raana has found an alternate career path in teaching science and literature to middle and high school kids.

Currently settled in the diverse city of Houston, Texas, with her lovely family, Dr. Raana finds joy and solace in the realms of painting and poetry when she's not working.

Becoming a published author has always been on her bucket list. With her debut book, set against the grand Himalayan range in the northern belt of Pakistan, she hopes to take her readers on an exhilarating journey of thrills and mysteries, weaving tales of nonstop action that will captivate their imagination and leave them on the edge of their seats.

Printed in the USA
CPSIA information can be obtained
at www.ICGtesting.com
LVHW092337281024
794794LV00002B/252